THE HOUSE BY THE RIVER

THE HOUSE BY THE RIVER

by

A P Herbert

Dales Large Print Books
Long Preston, North Yorkshire,
BD23 4ND, England.

British Library Cataloguing in Publication Data.

Herbert, A P
   The house by the river.

      A catalogue record of this book is
      available from the British Library

      ISBN   1-84262-365-6 pbk

Published in Large Print 2005 by arrangement with
House of Stratus

Dales Large Print is an imprint of Library Magna Books Ltd.

Printed and bound in Great Britain by
T.J. (International) Ltd., Cornwall, PL28 8RW

CHAPTER I

The Whittakers were At Home every Wednesday. No one else in Hammerton Chase was officially At Home at any time. So everyone went to the Whittakers' on Wednesdays.

There are still a few intimate corners in London where people, other than the poor, are positively acquainted with their neighbours. And Hammerton Chase is one of these. In heartless Kensington we know more of our neighbours than we may gather from furtive references to the Red Book and *Who's Who*, or stealthy reconnaissances from behind the dining-room curtains as he goes forth in the morning to his work and his labour. Our communication with him is limited to the throwing back over the garden-wall of his children's balls, aeroplanes, and spears, or – in the lowest parts of Kensington – to testy hammerings with the fire-irons towards the close of his musical evenings. Overt, deliberate, avoidable, social intercourse with any person living in the same street or the same block of mansions is a thing unknown. What true Londoner remembers going to an At Home, a dance, a musical evening, or other entertainment in his own street? Who is there who regards with friendship the occupant of the opposite flat?

Hammerton Chase could scarcely be regarded as a street. A short half-mile of old and dignified houses, clustered irregularly in all shapes and sizes along the sunny side of the Thames, with large trees and little gardens fringing the bank across the road, and, lying opposite, the Island, a long triangle of young willows, the haunt of wild duck and heron and swan – it had a unique, incomparable character of its own. It was like neither street, nor road, nor avenue, nor garden, nor any other urban unit of place in London or indeed, it was locally supposed, in the world. It had something, perhaps, of an old village and something of a Cathedral Close, something of Venice and something of the sea. But it was *sui generis*. It was the The Chase, W6. And the W6 was generally considered to be superfluous.

But, whatever it was, it prided itself on the intimate and sociable relations of its members. They were all on friendly terms with each other, and knew exactly the circumstances and employment, the ambitions, plans, and domestic crisis of each other at any given moment. They 'dropped in' at each other's houses for conversation and informal entertainment; they borrowed wine-glasses for their dinner-parties and tools for their gardens and anchors for their boats. They were a community, a self-sufficient community, isolated geographically from their natural homes in Chelsea and Kensington, W, by the dreary wilderness of West Kensington and the barbarous expanse of Hammersmith, and clinging almost pathetically together in their little oasis of civilization.

And yet they were not suburban. They were in physical fact on the actual borders of London County; they were six miles from Charing Cross. But Ealing and the suburbs are farther still. And the soul of Ealing was many leagues removed from the soul of The Chase, which, like The Chase, was something not elsewhere to be discovered.

So that on Wednesdays the Whittakers were At Home in the evening, and every one went. Andrew Whittaker was an artist and art-critic; though for various reasons he devoted more time to criticism than to execution. Mrs Whittaker wrote novels in the intervals of engaging a new servant or dismissing an old one, and grappling undaunted with the domestic crisis which either operation produced. They were both exceedingly pleasant, cultivated, and feckless people, and they well represented the soul of The Chase. Indeed, no one else was so well fitted to collect the bodies of The Chase together on Wednesdays.

On this Wednesday there were fewer bodies than usual in the grey drawing-room. It was a moist and thunderous evening, very heavy and still, and many of The Chase were gasping quietly in their own little gardens, reluctant to enter a house of any kind. And there were one or two households vaguely 'away in the country.' It was rather the habit of true members of The Chase to 'go away' in May, or in June, or in any month but August, not simply because it was a wise and sensible thing to do, August being an overrated and tumultuous month in the country, nor only because if you lived in the airy Chase the common craving of Londoners to escape from London in August did not affect you, but chiefly because if you lived in The Chase that was the kind of thing you did.

Mrs Whittaker was a little distressed by the meagre attendance. Six or seven ladies of The Chase, Mr Dimple, the barrister, Mr Mard, the architect, and his wife were there; but these were all elderly and unexciting, and without some powerful stimulus from the outer world it was impossible to prevent them from discussing food and domestic servants. Domestic worries dominated their lives. Life in The Chase was one long domestic worry. And the great problem of Mrs Whittaker's At Homes was to prevent people from talking about servants, food, and domestic worries. Her method was to invite large numbers of artistic, literary, and otherwise interesting people from distant

London, who were apparently immune from domestic worries or were at any rate capable of excluding them from their conversation. The artistic element was thinly represented this evening by a psychologist from Oxford and a dramatic critic. But, nobly though they strove to discuss the drama and the mind, they were hopelessly swamped by a loud discussion on domestic servants and food among the ladies of The Chase, vigorously led by Mrs Vincent and Mrs Church. Mrs Ralph Vincent was a carroty-haired lady of extraordinary aggressiveness and defiant juvenility in the face of her forty-five summers and seven children. Mrs Church was the widow-daughter of old Mrs Ambrose, who was ninety and extremely deaf. Mrs Church herself had an unfortunate stutter. Yet these two ladies, living together at Island View, practically constituted the Intelligence Staff of The Chase. They knew everything. They never went out, except on Wednesdays to the Whittakers', when the indomitable Mrs Ambrose strode unaided under the splendid elms to Willow House and laboured by stages up the narrow stairs. But their agents came to them daily for teas and 'little talks,' and handed over, willingly or no, the secrets of The Chase. Nor could it be said that either of them knew more or less than the other. Old Mrs Ambrose prided herself on her lip-reading, and no doubt Mrs

Church's unfortunate impediment made it easier for the old lady to practise this art to advantage. Some said, indeed, that Mrs Church's stutter had been assumed in filial piety for this very purpose.

Mrs Ambrose as busily endeavouring to read the lips of the psychologist and the dramatic critic, whom she suspected of being engaged in a discussion of unusual interest, if not actual indelicacy. People who knew of her supposed gift felt sometimes very uncomfortable about conversation in her presence, especially if they were speaking to some reckless person who did not know of it.

The voice of the psychologist was heard protesting to his host the sincerity and thoroughness of the Oxford method. Whittaker stood patiently in front of him with a trayful of home-made cocktails. 'We *make* them concentrate ... *a priori* ... processes of thought ... lectures ... philosophy ... system...'

Then domesticity broke out again, and Mrs Whittaker, listening with one ear to each party, raged furiously within. 'Mary takes the children in the morning ... the gas-oven ... margarine ... the geyser ... the front door-step ... pull out the damper ... simply walked out of the house ... margarine ... Mrs Walker's Bureau ... butter ... very good references ... margarine ... the principles of reasoning ... what about Susan? ... margarine ... a month's wages ... margarine ... thought-circles ... washing-up ... lady-help ... margarine...'

Mrs Whittaker despaired. Were none of her artistic circle coming? She went over to her husband and whispered fiercely, 'Are the Byrnes coming? Go out and ring them up. Tell them they simply *must.*'

Whittaker deposited his tray in the arms of the psychologist and went out; the psychologist assumed the air of one who is equal to any emergency, and sat solemnly embracing the tray.

When Whittaker came back there was a wide grin on his pleasant face. He announced:

'The Byrnes are coming in a minute – and he's bringing the Choir.'

'Oh, *good*,' said Mrs Whittaker, and echoing approvals came from several of the company.

The psychologist said, 'Is that *Stephen* Byrne?' in an awed voice, and tried not to look as impressed and gratified as he felt when Whittaker assured him that it was. The elderly ladies looked more cheerful, and abandoned the barren topic of domestic worries to discuss poetry and Mr Byrne. Mrs Ambrose said, 'I *like* Mr Byrne'; Mrs Church said, 'A *nice* man, Mr Byrne'; Mrs Vincent said, 'Such a *nice* couple, the Byrnes.'

There were many accomplished people living in The Chase, but Stephen Byrne was the lion of them all; there were many delightful people living in The Chase, but Stephen Byrne was the darling of them all. He was the gem, the treasure of The Chase. Indeed, he was the treasure of England. He was a real poet. Men had heard of him before the war; but it was in the years of war that he had come to greatness. He was one of a few men who had been able in a few fine poems to set free for the nation a little of the imprisoned grandeur, the mute emotion of that time. But none of all those young men, who found their voices suddenly in the war and spoke with astonishment the splendid feelings of the people, had so touched the imagination, had so nearly expressed the tenderness of England, as Stephen Byrne. At twenty-seven he was a great man – a national idol.

No wonder, therefore, that The Chase delighted in him. But there was more. He was personally delightful. So many successful men are unusually ugly, or unusually bad-tempered, or soured, or boorish, or intolerably rude; and the people of The Chase, being essentially a critical people and far too noble to be capable of intellectual snobbery, would not have given their hearts to a successful poet if he had been ugly or boorish or intolerably rude. Stephen Byrne was none of these things – but handsome and affable and beautifully mannered. And so they loved him.

While they were waiting for him it grew dark and a little cooler, and more of The Chase came in. Mr Dunk, the American, came in, and Petway, of the Needlework Guild, and Morrison, the publisher. After them came Mr and Mrs Stimpson. Stimpson was a Civil Servant, but his lifework was cabinet-making. Mrs Stimpson was an execrable housekeeper and mother, but knitted with extraordinary finish. Knitting was her craft; cabinet-making was her husband's craft. Everybody had a craft of some kind in The Chase. They all made things or did things, which nobody made or did in Kensington.

Sometimes this making or doing was their profession; sometimes it was a *parergon* carried on deliciously in leisure hours. In either case it was the most important part of their lives. Mr Dunk kept rabbits; Mr Farraday kept boats, and sailed interminably in his cutter or rowed about in an almost invisible dinghy. However innocent and respectable they looked, each of them, one felt, was capable of secret pottery, or privately addicted to modelling or engraving. There was nothing The Chase could not do.

When these people came in the At Home brightened appreciably; there was a loud noise of really intelligent conversation, and Mrs Whittaker was satisfied. Whittaker

17

laboured assiduously at his home-made cocktails, and was suitably rewarded by their rapid consumption. Whittaker's cocktails had the advantages and the defects of an impromptu composition, which is precisely what they were. He was bound by no cast-iron rules as to ingredients in manufacture. But they were always powerful and generally popular; and most of the ladies attempted them if only because they were such a glorious gamble. Only Mrs Ambrose resolutely declined. And as they drank them they were all pleasurably excited by the imminent advent of Stephen Byrne.

The door opened violently, striking the psychologist in the middle of the back, and a wave of people surged into the room, with much chattering and loud laughter. Towering in the centre of the mob was a huge clergyman, with large, round spectacles and a brick-red face, who reminded one instantly of Og, Gog, and Magog, however vague one's previous impressions of those personages had been. He had a voice like a Tube train, rumbling far off in a tunnel, and his laugh was like the bursting of shells. He was six foot eight, and magnificently proportioned. With him was a man of about twenty-seven, a Civil Servant and resident of The Chase, by name John Egerton. In front of these two, hopelessly dwarfed by the Rev. Peter, were two young ladies – and

Stephen Byrne, a tall figure in a black velvet smoking jacket.

It said much for the personality, and indeed the person, of the young poet that in the arresting presence of the Rev. Peter most of the company looked immediately at Stephen Byrne. Many of them, indeed, thought it more seemly for some reason to conceal their interest, and went on talking or listening to their neighbours; they swivelled their eyes painfully towards the door without moving their heads, and suddenly said 'Quite' or 'Really' with a vain affectation of intelligence and usually in an inappropriate context.

These were mostly men, who could not be expected openly to admit that there was present a more important male than themselves. But most of the women, and especially the elder ones, regarded with evident admiration the black-haired, bonny celebrity of Hammerton Chase. It was very black, that hair, unbelievably black, and of a curious, attractive texture. One wanted to touch it. And, although he was a poet, it was not too long.

Smiling happily under the light, Stephen Byrne was very good to look at. A high brow gave him a perhaps spurious suggestion of nobility, for the rest of the face was not so noble. The modern habit is to affix a label to every man, and be affronted if he forgets or ignores his label. But the most inveterate labeller would have been puzzled by the face of Stephen Byrne. In repose it was a handsome, impressive face, full of what is vaguely described as 'breeding,' the nose straight and thin, the mouth firm and unobtrusive. One felt confidence, sympathy, attraction. But when he spoke or smiled, one thought again. There was attraction still, and for most people an immediate irresistible charm, but less confidence. There was a certain weakness in the mobile mouth, a certain fleshliness. You could imagine this young man being noble or mean, cruel or kind, good-humoured or petulant, selfish or magnanimous or simply damnable. Which is merely to say that he was a complicated affair. But if indeed he had a darker side, it had never been revealed to the people of The Chase; and they loved him.

The two ladies were Margery Byrne, his wife, and Muriel Tarrant, a favourite niece of the Reverend Peter. They were both very fair, both very delightful without being exactly beautiful. Miss Muriel Tarrant was the sole unmarried and still marriageable maiden in The Chase. It was a curious thing; the female population of The Chase consisted almost entirely of married ladies, young or old, elderly ladies who were past that sort of thing, and small children. Muriel Tarrant swam like a solitary comet in this galaxy of fixed or immature stars. None could imagine why she remained single for a moment, so young and fresh and admirable she was. People indeed said that John Egerton... But no one knew.

Muriel's young brother, George Edwin, a tall youth with the precise features of a Greek sculpture and the immaculate locks of a barber's assistant, brought up the rear, looking a little dazed.

There was a third young lady, disconcertingly tall and slightly abashed, and an obviously artistic youth in a blue collar, clinging timidly to the skirts of the party – both strangers to The Chase.

Stephen Byrne introduced them.

'All these people,' he explained, with a comprehensive gesture, 'do pottery and engraving. They are The Chase. Give me one of your cocktails, Whittaker. No – give me two.'

With two thin glasses of Whittaker's latest concoction he walked over to old Mrs Ambrose, watching him from her distant corner and wishing she was less old and less deaf, so that she could command the attentions of pleasant and distinguished young men. When he came to her she glowed with contentment like the harvest moon emerging from a mist, and to her own intense astonishment and the horror of her daughter was prevailed upon by Stephen to accept and actually consume the cocktail he had brought her. So excited was she, and so excited was Mrs Church, her daughter, that Mrs Church's stutter became altogether unconquerable, and the old lady's lip-reading became more than ever an adventure in guesswork. This meant a complete breakdown in their system of communications, which made conversation difficult. But Stephen chattered and sparkled undeterred, and the old ladies chuckled and crooned with satisfaction. Mrs Ambrose thought he was talking about domestic servants, because she had lipread the word 'cook.' In fact, he was talking nonsense about the origin of the word *cock*-tail, as Mrs Church kept trying to explain. But she never got further than, 'He d – d – didn't say c – c – *cook*, Mother – he said c – c – c–' because the old lady always interrupted with 'Housemaids, ah – yes,' and wagged her white head with profound meaning.

The rumour travelled round the noisy room that Mr Byrne had made Mrs Ambrose have a cocktail, and they all said, 'How *like* him! the naughty old thing! No one else would have done that.' Margery Byrne was trying to make the dramatic critic talk about the drama, but he had come to the conclusion that no one in Hammerton liked to talk about anything but domestic worries. As he lived in a service flat and did not have any, it was far from easy for him, but he was doing his best, and had ascertained from Mrs Byrne that she had just engaged a new maid, named Emily, who seemed likely to be satisfactory. When Mrs Byrne heard of her husband's feat, she looked across at him fondly, but almost reproachfully. 'That means he's had three himself,' she said, with a gay laugh. The dramatic critic, who flattered himself that he had probed the depths of human nature, thought, 'What a nice, easygoing wife!' But Mrs Byrne was really thinking, 'I *wish* he wouldn't drink so many – horrid, strong stuff.'

And she saw that, though her husband was being so pleasant and kind to the two old ladies, he was looking most of the time at Muriel Tarrant, the pretty girl in the corner beyond him, who was talking to John Egerton, and blushing prettily about something.

Margery Byrne said to herself, 'I am not jealous,' and looked away.

An enormous chatter filled the room. The psychologist sat silent, noticing things. Mr Whittaker fussed about with coffee and thin glasses. Odd corners of tables and mantelpieces and bookshelves became crowded with discarded coffee-cups and dissipated glasses, perilously poised. Mrs Whittaker, talking busily to the Reverend Peter, listened anxiously, with both ears at the public pulse, as it were, and could detect no single murmur of domestic worries. Every one, it seemed, was being interesting and intelligent.

Then the carroty-haired Mrs Vincent bustled up to her. '*Won't* you make them sing to us, Mrs Whittaker? – Mr Byrne's Choir, I mean. I've never heard them, you know.'

The Reverend Peter roared across the room, 'A song, Stephen – a song! Forward, the Choir!'

The Hammerton Choir was the unduly dignified title of the faintly flippant, faintly musical company of pleasant people which the Byrnes gathered periodically at their house along The Chase. They sang, indeed, informally and wholly impromptu, a wide range of quartettes and choruses and glees. But volume of sound rather than delicacy of execution was their strong point, and the prevailing tone was frivolous. Indeed, it was scarcely in keeping with the sonorous title they had assumed; and Mrs Vincent and others of Mrs Whittaker's guests, who had heard of the Hammerton Choir, but had not actually heard it, might be pardoned if they had formed too flattering an impression of its powers.

Some of the Choir showed a certain bashfulness at the proposal that they should sing so publicly. John Egerton at first definitely refused, partly perhaps because he was happily occupied with Miss Muriel Tarrant

in an almost impregnable corner. She, however, not wishing the company to suppose
that she had any such thought, urged him
into the arena; and Stephen Byrne prevailed
upon the rest of his following. He himself
showed no signs of bashfulness.

Miss Tarrant was the Choir's principal
treble, and Stephen, bowing gallantly,
escorted her with Miss Tiffany to the piano,
a decayed and tinny instrument, with many
photographs of children obliquely regarding
each other on the top. Stephen sat at the
piano, and the Reverend Peter stood stooping like a tired steeple beyond. He was, of
course, the bass. The young man with the
blue collar provided with John Egerton a
throaty and wavering tenor. Egerton tried to
stand next to Miss Tarrant, but was thwarted
without intention by his companion tenor.
Miss Tiffany grew slowly pinker and pinker.
A solemn hush descended. The company
held their breath.

At the beginning of the Great War Mr
Asquith made a speech. In it he formulated
the principles for which this nation was
fighting. The formula was perfect and
worthy of a great master of formulae, sonorous and dignified, yet not verbose. It said
everything without saying a word too much.
And Mr Asquith was, justifiably, so pleased
with it that for many years he lost no
opportunity of publicly repeating it, or, if he

did not repeat it, of reminding people about it in speeches and pronouncements and letters to the Press. It began, 'We shall not sheathe the sword,' and for a long time it was blazoned on every hoarding. Few men can have had so striking a literary success with four sentences.

But over and above its conciseness and majesty and lucidity the formula had other qualities which may or may not have been consciously imparted to it by Mr Asquith. Its component sentences had the literary form of Hebraic poetry, the structure and rhythm of the Psalms. They might, indeed, have come out of the Psalms.

But this was not all. One would understand the Prime Minister of England modelling some important literary composition on the style of the Psalms, which is a noble style. And that being so, one could understand the result being more or less easily adjustable to some one or other of those Church of England chants, which have done so much to popularise the Psalms of David. But the extraordinary thing about Mr Asquith's formula was that it fitted exactly the Quadruple Chant, the unique and famous Quadruple Chant, designed by a benignant Church to make the longest Psalm that David composed less inexpressibly fatiguing than it would be to the music of a miserable single or double chant. There were four sentences in Mr Asquith's formula. There were four musical sentences in the Quadruple Chant, each divided in twain. And they fitted each other like a glove, or, rather, like a well-fitting glove. It was marvellous. The only reasonable conclusion was that Mr Asquith, in a moment of pious exaltation, had deliberately set his formula to the Quadruple chant.

Alone of the English-speaking race Stephen Byrne had discovered these astounding truths. Having formed the conclusion that Mr Asquith had written the words to that chant, he held that one ought to sing the words to that chant. This would be the highest compliment to the man and the best means of perpetuating his work. And so, with many others, he did. But there is a season for all things; and it cannot be pretended that Mrs Whittaker's select and crowded At Home was the season for this particular thing.

Stephen struck a chord. The company wondered what masterpiece was to be given them – perhaps some Schubert, perhaps something from Gilbert and Sullivan.

Then the great anthem rolled out. The voices of the Hammerton Choir were not individually of high quality, but they blended well, and their volume was surprising. They sang in excellent time, all stopping at the asterisks absolutely together, all accomplishing with perfect unanimity those long polysyllabic passages on one note which make psalm-singing in our churches so fruitful a source of precipitancy and schism.

'We shall not sheathe the sword' (pause for breath), 'which we hàve not/ lightly/ drawn, //until Belgium has recovered all* and MORE than/all that/she has/sacrificed.

'Until France is adequàte/ly sec/urèd //against the/ menace/of ag/gression.'

(The accentuation of *ate* in 'adequately' was the one blot on the pointing; it was unworthy of Mr Asquith.)

'Until the rights of the smaller nationàlit/ies of/ Europe// are placed upon an ùnnass/aila/ble found/ation/.'

(That was a grand stanza; the Hammerton singers gave a delicious burlesque of the country choir gabbling with evergrowing speed through the first words, and falling with a luxurious snarl on their objective, the unfortunate accented syllable *al*).

'And until the military dòmin/ation of/Prussia//is wholly and/final/ly dest/royèd.'

(*Prussia* was given with a splendid crescendo of hate, worthy of the best Prussian traditions, and 'destroy-èd' came with an effective rallentando.) The Reverend Peter Tarrant, rumbling in a profound bass the final 'destroy-èd,' was so life-like an imitation of a real clergyman leading a real village choir that those of the audience who had been slightly shocked by the whole performance became suddenly amused, and those who had not been shocked at all, which was a large majority, were reduced to the final stages of hysterical approval. The 'turn' was a huge success. A roar of laughter and clapping and questioning followed the solemn ending. The Choir were urged to 'do it again.' The two ladies, flushed and almost overcome by the applause, a circumstance quite new in the history of the Choir, begged to be excused; but Stephen once more constrained them. This time, closely following the best contemporary models on the variety stage, he urged the audience to assist, and produced from some mysterious source a number of copies of the words, neatly typed and pointed. And then, indeed, a wondrous thing was heard. For all that mixed but mainly respectable company rose up, and, opening timidly, rendered with an ever-increasing confidence and volume that profane and ridiculous hymn. Stephen Byrne stood superbly on a footstool and conducted with a poker, his black eyes flashing, his whole figure vital with excitement and mirth. And all those people were under his spell. Even the psychologist forbore for a moment to analyse the workings either of his own or any man's mind, and concentrated genuinely on the correct pointing of his words, chuckling insanely at each half-verse. All of them chuckled and gurgled as they sang.

But such is the hypnotic effect of any music with religious associations, and so powerful is the simple act of singing vigorously in unison as a generator of sentiment and solemnity in those who sing, that by the end of the third stanza they had forgotten that they were being funny, that the whole thing was a ridiculous joke, and discovered themselves, to Stephen's intense dismay, chanting with long faces and tones of inexpressible fervour the pious resolution that the military domination of Prussia must be wholly and finally 'destroy-èd.' They finished, almost with lumps in their throats, so moving was it all, and stood for a moment in a sheepish hush, half feeling that some one should say, 'Let us pray,' or give out a text before they might sit down. Then some one cackled in the background, and the spell was broken with peals of insane laughter.

While the hoarse company were having their glasses justifiably refilled, Margery Byrne came quickly up to her husband, and gave him the look which means to a husband, 'I want to go home now.' She was tired and she looked tired; and she was going to have a baby. Stephen said, 'Right you are, my dear – just a minute.' He was talking now to the Reverend Peter and Muriel Tarrant, who was prettily flushed and a little excited. He was arguing with the

Reverend Peter about the poetry of John Donne. He, too, was excited and pleased and reluctant to go home. But he knew that Margery ought to go home. And of such stuff are the real temptations of man.

He looked an apology and an appeal at his wife and said, 'One minute, my dear... Would you mind?' knowing well that she minded. Mrs Byrne said that of course she did not mind, and went back to her seat by the dramatic critic, yawning furtively.

So Stephen stood against the piano and defended John Donne, that strange Elizabethan mixture of piety and paganism and poetry and nastiness. He had forgotten Mr Asquith now; he had forgotten the Choir and Muriel Tarrant, and he was absorbed in the serious pronouncement of an artistic belief. The Reverend Peter said that he was no prig, but some of John Donne was too much for him. He could not believe in the essential greatness of a grown man who could write such stuff. Stephen began to quote a line or two from memory; then he reached up for an old brown volume on one of Whittaker's shelves and read from it in a low voice that only the clergyman could hear. 'This is what *I* make of him,' he said. And he began to talk. He talked with the real eloquence of a master of words profoundly moved, with growing earnestness and vigour. He spoke of the eternal contradictions of human personality, of the amazing mixtures which make up men; how true was the saying of Samuel Butler that everything a man does is in a measure a picture of himself, yet how true it was that one could not confidently judge what a man was like from what he wrote. He told the Reverend Peter that he was narrow in his estimate – unjust. One must strike a balance. Many of the company had gathered about him now, and were listening; Stephen saw this at last, and finished. Then the Reverend Peter laid a large hand affectionately on his shoulder and said, 'You're a wonderful man, Stephen. I surrender. I dare say I've wronged the fellow... I'll read him again... You poets are certainly an odd mixture.' And that was the thought of all those who had heard the singing and listened to the talk.

Stephen turned from him with a curious smile and saw suddenly the reproachful figure of his wife.

He said, 'Come along, my dear – I'm so sorry! Are you coming, John?'

Egerton looked across at Muriel Tarrant and her mother. They were entangled with Mrs Ambrose and showed no signs of escaping. He said, 'No – I shall stay a little, I think.'

In the hot darkness of The Chase Stephen took his wife's arm, and knew at once that she was cross. They walked in silence to The

32

House by the River and in silence entered the poky little hall. Stephen cursed himself; it was a stupid end to a jolly evening. In the hall he kissed her and said that he was sorry, and she sighed and smiled, and kissed him and went upstairs.

Stephen walked reflectively into the dining-room and mixed himself a whisky and water. And as he drank, Emily Gaunt came up from the kitchen to ask if Mrs Byrne wanted tea. Emily Gaunt was the new maid. Stephen finished his whisky and noticed for the first time that she was pretty – in a way.

'No, thank you, Emily.' he said, and smiled at her. And Emily smiled.

CHAPTER II

It was nearly high tide. Stephen Byrne stood at the end of his garden and regarded contentedly the River Thames. The warm glow of sunset lingered about the houses by Hammersmith Bridge and the tall trees on the Surrey side. The houses and the tall trees and the great old elms by William Morris' house stood rigid on their heads in the still water, and all that wide and comfortable reach between the Island and Hammersmith

Bridge was beautiful in the late sun. There were a few small clouds flushed with pink in the southern sky, and these also lay like reefs of coral here and there in the water. The little boats in the foreground, moored in ranks in the tiny roads off Hammerton Chase, lay already deep in the shadow of the high houses of the Terrace, and the water about them was cool and very black. The busy tugs went by, hurrying up with the last of the flood, long chains of barges swishing delightfully behind them. The tug *Maud* went by, and *Margaret*, her inseparable companion. On their funnels were a green stripe and a red stripe and a yellow stripe. On their barges were reposeful bargees, smoking old pipes in the stern, and pondering, no doubt, the glories of their life. *Margaret* this evening had a glorious barge, a great black vessel with a light blue line along the gunwale and a tangle of rigging and coffee-coloured sails strewn along her deck. As they fussed away past the Island the long waves crept smoothly across the river and stole secretly under the little boats in the roads, the sailing-boats and the rowing-boats and the motor-boats and the absurd dinghies, and tossed them up and heaved them about with pleasing chuckles; and went on to the garden-wall of the houses and splashed noisily under Stephen's nose and frothed back to the boats. And the boats rolled happily with charming ripply noises till the water was calm and quiet again. A swan drifted lazily backwards with the tide, searching for something in the back of its neck. It was all very soothing and beautiful, and Stephen Byrne could have looked at the high tide for ever.

High tide was a great moment at Hammerton Chase. It had a powerful influence on the minds of The Chase. There was a tremendous feeling of fulfilment, of achievement, about the river when the flood was sweeping up, wandering on to the road on one bank and almost topping the towpath on the other, making Hammerton Reach a broad and dignified affair. The time went quickly when the tide was high. They were long hours when the tide was low, when the river dwindled to a mean and dejected stream, creeping narrowly along between gloomy stretches of mud, and brickbats and broken crockery, where the boats lay protesting and derelict in uncomfortable attitudes. There was a sense of disappointment then, of stagnation and failure. Those who lived by the river and loved and studied it were keenly susceptible to the tides.

And this tide seemed particularly copious and good. For one thing he had dined well. He had drunk at Brierley's a satisfying quantity of admirable Château Yquem, followed by some quite excellent old brandy. He was by no means drunk; but he was conscious of a glow, a warm contentment. Life seemed amicable and prosperous and assured. After all, he was a fortunate young fellow, Stephen Byrne. The life of a successful poet was undoubtedly a good life.

And he was happily married. His wife was pretty and loving and almost perfect. Very soon she was to have another baby; and it would be a boy, of course. The first was a dear, delightful, incomparable creature, but she was a girl. The next would be a boy.

And he loved his home. He loved Hammersmith and the faithful companionable river, the barges and the jolly tugs and his little garden and his motor-boat and his dinghy and the sun-steeped window-seat in the corner of his study, the white conservatory he had whitewashed with his wife, and the exuberant creeper they had trained together.

Stephen's house was The House by the River, which stood with one other in an isolated communion between Hammerton Terrace and the Island. The bank swung out widely above the Terrace, so that Stephen's house and its neighbour were on a miniature promontory, commanding unobstructed the ample curve of the river to Hammersmith Bridge, a mile away. The houses were old and ill-appointed within, with rattling sashes and loose doors, but dignified and beautiful without, modest old brick draped generously with green. And they were full of tall windows drinking in the sun and looking away to the south towards the hills about Putney and Roehampton, or westwards to the remote green of Richmond Hill. They were rich with sunshine and an air that was not London's.

Stephen looked up at his high old house and was proud of it. He was proud of the thick ivy and creeper all over it and the green untidy garden below it, and the pretty view of the dining-room, where the light was on, a lonely island of gold in the dusk, seen delightfully through matted ropes of creeper.

There was a light in the bathroom, too – Emily Gaunt, the housemaid, no doubt, having a bath. As he looked up he heard the sound of water tumbling down the pipes outside the house, and deduced absently that Emily had pulled up the waste-plug.

Stephen looked over his neighbour's wall into his neighbour's garden. His neighbour was John Egerton and a good friend of his, probably the best friend he had. But John Egerton was not in his garden. Stephen was sorry, for he felt that inclination towards human society which normally accompanies the warm afterglow of good wine. Mrs Byrne was dining with her mother, and would not be back for an hour or so. Stephen regretted that he had come back so early. He could not write. He did not want to read. He felt full, but not capable, of poetry. He wanted company. The glow was still upon him, but it was growing chilly on the wall. It was time to go in. He knocked out his pipe. The dottle fell with a fizzle in the water.

He walked in slowly to the dining-room and poured out a glass of port. Failing company there must be more glow. The port was good and admirably productive of glow. Stephen stood by the old oak sideboard, luxuriously reviving the sensations of glow. The dining-room, it seemed to him, was extraordinarily beautiful; the sea picture by Quint an extraordinarily adequate picture of the sea; the port extraordinarily comforting and velvety; the whole of life extraordinarily well arranged.

When he had finished the port he heard a timid creaking on the staircase. He went into the tiny hall, walking with a self-conscious equilibrium. Emily Gaunt was coming down the stairs to her bedroom, fresh from her bath. Emily Gaunt was a pleasant person, well-proportioned, and, for a housemaid, unusually fair to see. Her eyes, like her hair, were a very dark brown, and there was a certain refinement in her features. Her hair was hanging about her shoulders and her face – usually pale – was rosy from her bath. In the absence of a dressing-gown or a kimono, she wore an old coat of Cook's over her night-gown. Cook was skinny and Emily was plump, so that Cook's coat was far from meeting where it ought to have met. There was a great deal of Emily's neck and Emily's night-gown to be seen.

Stephen, so far, had taken little notice of Emily, except that one evening he had smiled at her for some reason and she had smiled at him; but at this moment, in the special circumstances of this lovely evening, she seemed in his eyes surprisingly desirable. In the half-light from the dining-room it was easy to forget that she was a servant. She was merely a warm young female creature, plump and comely, and scantily clad.

And there was no one else in the house.

'Good evening, Emily,' said Stephen, looking up the stairs.

'Good evening, Mr Byrne,' said Emily, halting on the stairs. She was a little surprised to see him. Cook was having her 'evening out' and Emily had thought herself alone in the house.

Now, Emily Gaunt was a well-behaved young woman. She was accustomed to being looked at by her male employers, and she was accustomed to keeping them at a proper distance. For so she had been brought up. But when she was not looked at she was usually sensible of a certain disappointment. Stephen Byrne had not looked at her enough, and she was undeniably disappointed. She liked the look of him; she liked his voice when he said, 'Where are my boots, please, Emily?' And she did not get on well with Mrs Byrne. Moreover, she had had a warm bath and was conscious also of a kind of glow.

So that when she had said, 'Good evening, Mr Byrne,' she continued at once her demure and unaffected descent. Cook would have turned and fled up the stairs, panting with modesty. So would many another domestic young person.

But Emily descended. If she had waited, or turned back up the stairs, or faltered, 'Oh, Sir,' and scurried like a young hind away from him, there is no doubt that Stephen would have made himself scarce – would have left the coast clear.

But she descended. When she came to the bottom of the stairs where Stephen was standing, there was hardly space for her to pass. Stephen made no move. He said fatuously, 'Had a nice bath, Emily?' and he put one arm around her as she passed, lightly, almost timidly, just touching the back of Cook's coat.

Emily said, 'Yes, thank you, sir,' and looked at him. Only a glance, quick and furtive as an electric spark – but what a glance! Yet she made no attempt to stop; she did not giggle or stammer or protest; she passed on. In another moment she would have gone.

But Stephen had touched her. He had received and registered that naughty and electrical glance. He was inflamed.

He did a thing the like of which he had never done before. He closed his right arm about the girl and firmly embraced her. And he kissed her very suddenly and hotly.

Emily screamed.

Stephen pulled her closer and kissed her again. And again Emily screamed. It was all very unfortunate. For it may be that if he had been less precipitate he could have been equally amorous without encountering anything more than a purely formal opposition. Emily Gaunt was prepared to be kissed, but not suddenly, not violently. It should have been properly led up to – a little talk, a compliment or two, some blushes, and a delicate embrace. That was the proper routine in Emily's set, or in anybody else's set for that matter. But this sudden, desperate, hot-breathed entanglement was quite another thing. It was frightening. And who can blame Emily Gaunt for that high-pitched rasping cry?

Stephen blamed her. It startled him a little, that screaming – frightened him, too. It brought him back to reality. He thought suddenly of neighbours, of John Egerton, of old Mrs Ambrose across the way. Suppose they heard. It became urgent to stop the screaming. Playfully, almost, he put his hands at Emily's throat. And even the touch of her throat was somehow inflammatory. It made him want to kiss her again.

'Shut up, you little fool,' he said. 'I shan't hurt you.' But Emily's nerve had gone. She opened her mouth to scream again. Stephen's hands tightened about the neck and the scream was never heard. *'Now,* will you be quiet?' he said. 'You're perfectly safe, Emily – I'm sorry... I was a fool...' and he released his grip.

But Emily was thoroughly, hideously, frightened now. A kind of despairing wail, a thin and inarticulate 'Help!' came from her. Stephen put his hand over her mouth, and Emily bit him.

And then Stephen saw red. The lurking animal which is in every man was already strong in him that evening, though Emily's first scream had cowed it a little. Now it took complete charge. With a throaty growl of exasperation he put both hands at the soft throat of Emily and shook her, jerkily exhorting her as he did so, 'Will – you – be quiet – you – silly – little fool – will – you – be quiet – you – fool – you'll – have – everybody – here – you...'

He only meant to shake her – he did not mean to squeeze with his hands – did not know that he *was* squeezing – mercilessly. He was between Emily and the dining-room, and in the dim light of the hall he could not see the starting, horrible eyes, the darkening flesh of poor Emily Gaunt. He only knew that this silly screaming was intolerable and must be stopped – stopped for certain, without further bother ... before the whole street came round ... before his wife came back ... before... 'Stop it, will you?... For God's sake, stop it!' he cried, almost plaintively, as his grip loosened a moment, and a strangled gasp burst from Emily. He was too much possessed with his anxious rage to notice *how* strangled it was. What he wanted was silence ... complete silence, that was it ... screams and gasps, they were all dangerous... 'Oh ... stop it ... can't you?'

The shaking process had taken them across the tiny hall. They were by the hat-stand now. Emily's oscillating head cannoned against a hat-peg. Her weight became suddenly noticeable. Emily's hands stopped scrabbling at his wrists ... her bare feet stopped kicking. Good, she was becoming sensible. Thank God! Cautiously, with a vast relief, Stephen took his hands away. 'That's better,' he said.

And then Emily Gaunt fell heavily against his shirtfront and slithered past him to the floor. Her forehead hit the bottom corner of the hat-stand. Her body lay limp, face downwards, and perfectly still.

In the dark hall the sound of snoring was heard.

He knew then that Emily Gaunt was dead. But it was absurd... He turned on the light, groping stupidly in the dark for the switch. His hands were shaking – that was from the gripping, of course. And they were sweating. So was his face.

Kneeling down, he pulled at Emily's shoulders. He pulled her over on to her back.

'My God!' he whispered. 'My God! ... my God!...'

A bell jangled in the basement. Someone with his head lowered was peering through the frosted glass of the front door.

CHAPTER III

In moments of crisis the human mind can become extraordinarily efficient. Before the bell was silent in the basement, the mind of Stephen Byrne, kneeling in a sweat by the dead body of a housemaid, had covered a vast field of circumstance and performed two or three distinct logical processes. His first instinct was to put out the light. With that person peering on the doorstep the light in the hall had better be out. He felt exposed, naked, illuminated. On the other hand, one could see practically nothing through the frosted glass from outside, only the shadow of anyone actually moving in the hall. That he knew from experience. Probably the person – whoever it was – could see nothing that was on the floor, nothing that was below the level of his or her interfering eye. If Stephen stayed still as he was, the person might never know he was there, might even go away in disgust. To put the light out would be a gratuitous advertisement that somebody was in the house. Besides, it would look so rude.

Stephen did not turn out the light. He knelt there on two knees and a hand, staring like a snake at the front door. With his right hand he was stealthily scratching his left armpit. It was itching intolerably. And his dress collar was sticking into his neck. He was intensely conscious of these things.

But all the time the precipitate arguments were jostling in his brain. What sort of person would peer through the glass? Surely a very familiar thing to do. He could think of a few people who would do it – the Whittakers – but they were away; his wife – but it was too early, and she had a latch-key; John Egerton – but Stephen thought he was out. Or a policeman, of course.

A policeman who had heard the screaming, or been told of the screaming, might do it, or even a neighbouring busybody, if he had heard. But they would have clattered up to the door, run up or stopped importantly on the doorstep – probably hammered with the knocker. The person had not done that. He had only rung that damnable bell.

The person's head disappeared. He gave a loud knock with the big brass knocker which Stephen had bought in Jerusalem. Just one knock. Then the whole world was silent. Stephen's heart thumped like a steam-engine going at slow speed. He thought, 'It's true what they say in the books ... I can hear it.'

The person shuffled its feet on the step.

'My God!' said Stephen again. 'My God!'

In the hall there was an enormous silence. A tug hooted dismally on the river. Stephen started scratching again. He was thinking of his wife now, of Margery. He loved Margery – he loved her very truly and well. And she was just going to have a baby. What would she– How would she– O God!

But she must not know. He would do something in a minute, when the damned fool had gone away. Why the hell didn't he go away, and leave a man alone? It must be some kind of visitor – not a policeman, or a panicky neighbour. They would have been more impatient. Why the hell didn't he go? It was Whittaker, perhaps. Or that South American chap.

The person did not go away. For the person had only been in the doorstep for thirty seconds in all, and the person was in no hurry.

Soon he would go away – he must go away, Stephen thought. The *hours* he had been out there. It must be a long time, because Stephen's knees were so sore. And he did want to get on with doing something – he was not clear what – but something. 'God will provide,' he thought.

And as he uttered that hideous blasphemy the person began to whistle. He whistled gently an air from *I Pagliacci*, and to Stephen Byrne it was merciful music. For it was a favourite tune of John Egerton's, bawled often by both of them at casual gatherings of the Hammerton Choir in Mrs Byrne's drawing-room. It must be John, after all, this person on the doorstep; good old John – thank God! If it was John, he would let him in; he would tell him the whole story. John must help him.

It was suddenly revealed to Stephen that he could not bear this burden alone. It was too much. John was the man.

But one must be careful. One must make sure. A cunning look came into his eyes. With elaborate stealth he crawled backwards from Emily's body and so into Emily's bedroom, which looked over the street. Under the blind he reconnoitred the front doorstep. The back of the person was turned towards him, but it was clear to him that the person was John Egerton, though he could only see part of the back and nothing of the head. No two persons in Hammerton Chase, or probably in the world, wore a shabby green coat like that. It was certainly John, come round for some singing, no doubt. He walked back boldly into the hall. He was cooler now, and his heart was working more deliberately. But he was horribly afraid. He put out the lights.

Then he opened the front door, very grudgingly, and looked round the corner.

'Hullo!' said Egerton.

'Hullo!' said Stephen. 'Come in,' and then, with a sudden urgency – '*quick!*'

John Egerton came slowly in and stood still in the dark.

'What's the matter?' he asked.

Stephen said, 'I'm in a hole,' and turned on the light.

It was very badly managed. No doubt he should have hidden Emily away before he opened the door; should have led up gradually to the ultimate revelation; should have carefully prepared a man like Egerton for a sight like the body of Emily Gaunt. For it was a coarse and terrible sight. She lay on her back by the hat-stand, with her dark hair tumbled on the floor, her face mottled and blue, her eyes gaping disgustingly, her throat marked and inflamed with the fingers of her employer. The coat of Cook was crumpled beneath her, and she had torn great rents in her night-dress in her desperate resistance, so that she lay half-naked in the cruel glare of the electric light. Her two plump legs were crossed fantastically like the legs of a crusader, but so that the feet were wide apart. Her pink flesh glistened and smelt powerfully of soap.

It was not the kind of thing to spring upon any man, least of all should it have been sprung upon Egerton. For he was a highly sensitive man and easily shocked. He had not been, like Stephen, to the war – being a Civil Servant and imperfect in the chest – and in an age when the majority of living young men have looked largely on, and become callous about, death, John Egerton had never seen a dead body.

And he was a person of extraordinary modesty, in the sense in which most women but few men possess modesty. He had a real chastity of thought which few men ever achieve. John Egerton was no prig. Only he had this natural purity of outlook which made him actually blush when indelicate things were said on the stage or hinted at in private society.

And now he was suddenly confronted in the house of his best friend with the dead and disgusting body of a half-naked female. He was inexpressibly shocked.

When the light went on and he looked down at the floor, his mouth opened suddenly, but he said no word; he only stared incredulously at the sprawling flesh.

Then he began to blush. A faint flush travelled slowly over his rather sallow face. He looked up then at Stephen, watching anxiously in the corner.

'What the devil–' he said.

From the tone in which he spoke, Stephen realised suddenly the error he had made. Pulling down a coat from a peg, he flung it over the body. Only a few times had he heard John Egerton speak like that and look like that, but he knew quite clearly what it meant. John should have been kept out of this. Or he should have had it broken to him. Of course. But there was no time – no time – that was the trouble. Stephen looked at his watch. It was twenty to ten. At any moment his wife might be back. Something must be done.

He opened the dining-room door. 'Come in here,' he said, and they went in.

John Egerton stood by the sideboard looking very grim and perplexed. He could not be called handsome, not at least beside Stephen Byrne. There was less intellect but more character in his face, a kind of moral refinement in the adequate jaw and steady grey eyes, set well apart under indifferent eyebrows. His face was pale from too much office-work, and he had the habit of a forward stoop, from peering nervously at new people. These things gave him, somehow, a false air of primness, and a little detracted from the kindliness, the humanity, which was the secret of his character and his charm. For ultimately men were charmed by John, though a deep-seated shyness concealed him from them at a first meeting. His voice was soft and unassuming, his mouth humorous, but firm. He had slightly discoloured teeth, not often visible. Stephen's teeth were admirable and flashed attractively when he smiled.

'What's it all mean?' John said. 'Is she–'

Stephen said, 'She's dead ... it's Emily, our maid.'

'How?' Egerton began.

'I – I was playing the fool ...pretended I was going to kiss her, you know ... the little fool thought I meant it ... got frightened ... then something ... I don't know what happened exactly ... she bumped her head... Oh, damn it, there's no time to explain ... we've got to get her away somehow ... and I want you to help ... Margery...'

'Get her away?' said John; 'but the police ... you can't...'

John Egerton was still far from grasping the full enormity of the position. He had been badly shocked by the sight of the body. He was shocked by his friend's incoherent confession of some vulgar piece of foolery with a servant. He was amazed that a man like Stephen should even 'pretend' that he was going to kiss a servant. That kind of thing was not done in The Chase, and Stephen was not that kind of man, he thought. No doubt he had had a little too much wine, flung out some stupid compliment or other; there had been a scuffle, and then some accident, a fall or something – the girl probably had a weak heart; fleshy people often did: it was all very horrible and regrettable, but not criminal. Nothing to be kept from the police.

But it was damnably awkward, of course, with Mrs Byrne in that condition. Stephen's spluttering mention of her name had suddenly reminded him of that. There would be policemen, fusses, inquests, and things. She would be upset. John had a great regard for Mrs Byrne. She oughtn't to be upset just now. But it couldn't be helped.

Stephen Byrne was pouring out port again – a full glass. He lifted and drank it with an impatient urgency, leaning back his black head. Some of the wine spilled out as he drank, and flowed stickily down his chin. Three drops fell on his crumpled shirt-front and swelled slowly into pear-shaped stains.

His friend's failure to understand was clearly revealed to him, and filled him with an unreasonable irritation. It was his own fault, of course. He should have told him the whole truth. But somehow he couldn't – even now – though every moment was precious. Even now he could not look at John and tell him simply what he had done. He took a napkin from the sideboard drawer and rubbed it foolishly across his shirt-front, as he spoke. He said: 'Oh, for God's sake, John ... don't you understand I ... I believe I ... I've killed her ... myself ... I don't know.' He looked quickly at John and away again. John's honest mouth was opening. His grey eyes were wide and horrified. When Stephen saw that, he hurried on, 'I may be wrong ... but anyhow Margery mustn't know anything about it ... you *must* see that ... it would probably kill her ... and she'll be back any moment now. Oh, *come* on, for God's sake.' A sudden vision of his wife walking through the front door on to that horrible thing in the hall spurred him to the door.

John Egerton stood still by the solid table, his hands gripping the edge of it behind him. He understood now.

'Good God!' he said quickly, as if to himself, and again, 'Good God!' Then, starting up, 'But, Stephen, it's ... it's ... you mean...' Suddenly the word 'murder' had flashed into his thoughts, and that word seemed to light up the whole ghastly business, made it immediately more hideous. 'It's *murder*,' he had been going to say, but some fantastic sense of delicacy stopped him.

Stephen halted at the door. A wild rage came over him. There was a strange kind of fierce resolution about him then which his friend had never seen before.

'Oh, for God's sake, don't stand dithering there, John,' he flung back. 'Are you going to help me or not? If not, clear out ... if you are, come on ... quick, before Margery comes.' He went into the hall.

John Egerton said no more, but followed. That illuminating unspoken word 'murder,' which had shown him the whole awfulness of this affair, had shown him also the urgency of the present moment, the necessity of helping Stephen to 'get her away.' For Margery Byrne's sake. Just how he felt towards Stephen at that moment, what he would have done if Stephen had been a bachelor, he had had no time to consider. And it did not matter. For Mrs Byrne's – for Margery's – sake, something must be done, as Stephen said. And he, John Egerton, must help.

'What are you going to do?' he said.

Stephen was crouched on his haunches, busily tidying Emily's night-dress, pulling it about.

'The river,' he said shortly. 'It's high tide– Thank God!' he added.

John Egerton looked shrinkingly at the torn and ineffective night-dress, at the wide spaces of pink flesh showing through the rents. He could not imagine himself picking up that body. He said, 'What? – like – like *that?*'

Stephen looked up. 'Yes,' he said; 'why

54

not?' But he knew very well why not. Because of a certain insane sense of decency which governs even a murderer in the presence of death. Emily Gaunt must not be 'got away' like that! Besides, it would be dangerous. He thought for a moment. Then, 'No,' he said. 'Wait a minute,' and clattered down the basement stairs.

When he came back he was trailing behind him a long and capacious sack, which had hung on a nail in the scullery for the receipt of waste paper and bottles and odds and ends of domestic refuse. The sack, fortunately, had been only half full. All its contents he had tumbled recklessly on the scullery floor. But as he came up the stairs he was curiously disturbed by the thought of that refuse. What was to be done with it? What would Margery say? The scullery had been recently cleaned out, he knew. And the sack? How would he explain its disappearance? These damned details.

'Here you are,' he said. 'This will do,' and he laid the sack on the floor.

He began to put Emily into the sack. He drew the mouth of the sack over her feet. They were already cold. John Egerton stood stiffly under the light, in a kind of paralysis of disgust. He felt 'I must help!... I must help!' but somehow he could not move a finger.

The sack was over the knees now. It was strangely difficult. The toes kept catching.

But Stephen was fantastically preoccupied with the refuse on the scullery floor, with coming explanations about the sack. 'There'll be an awful row,' he said ... 'the hell of a mess down there ... what shall I say about the sack?' Then, suddenly, 'What shall I say, John?... Think of something, for God's sake!'

John Egerton jumped. The wild incongruity of Stephen's question scarcely occurred to him. He tried solemnly to think of something to say about the sack. He would be helpful here, surely. But no thought came. His mind was a confused muddle of nightdresses and inquests and naked legs and Margery Byrne – Margery Byrne arriving quietly on the doorstep – Margery Byrne scandalized, agonized, hideously, fatally ill.

'I don't know, Stephen,' he said feebly – 'I don't know say you ... oh, anything.'

He was fascinated now by the progress of the sack, which had nearly covered the legs. He saw clearly that a moment was coming when he would *have* to help, when one of them would have to lift Emily and one of them manipulate the sack. Already Stephen was cursing and in difficulties. The nightdress kept rucking up and had to be pulled back, and when that was done the sack lost ground again.

'Oh, hell!' he said, with a note of final exasperation, 'lend a hand, John – lift her a bit,' and then as John still hesitated, sick with reluctance, 'Oh, *lift* her, can't you?'

John stooped down. The moment had come. He put his hands under the small of Emily's back, shuddering as he touched her. With an effort he lifted her an inch or two. With a great heave Stephen advanced the sack six inches. Then it caught again in those maddening toes. With a guttural exclamation of rage he turned back towards the feet and tugged furiously at the sack. When it was free John Egerton had relaxed his hold. Emily was lying heavy on the slack of the sack. He was gazing with a kind of helpless horror at the purple inflammation of Emily's throat, realizing for the first time just how brutal and violent her end had been.

Stephen cursed again. 'Lift, damn you, *lift* – oh, hell!'

John lifted, and with a wild fumbling impatience the whole of Emily's body was covered. Only the head and one arm were left. They had forgotten the arm. It lay flung away from the body, half hidden under an overcoat. Stephen seized it savagely and tried to bend it in under the mouth of the sack with brutal ridiculous tugs, like an ill-tempered man packing an over-loaded bag. John watched him with growing disapproval.

'That's no good,' he said. 'Pull down the sack again.' Stephen did so. The sweat now was running down his face; he was spent and panting, and his composure was all gone. With his black hair ruffled over his forehead he looked wicked.

Something of his impatience had communicated itself to John, mastering even his abhorrence. He wanted furiously to get the thing done. It was he now who seized the recalcitrant arm and thrust it into the sack; it was he who fiercely pulled the sack over Emily's head, and hid at last that puffy and appalling face with a long 'Ah – h' of relief. At the mouth of the sack was a fortunate piece of cord, threaded through a circle of ragged holes.

John Egerton pulled it tight and fumbled at the making of a knot. He felt vaguely that something special in the way of knots was required – a bowline – a reef knot or something – not a 'granny,' anyhow. How was it you tied a reef knot? Dimly remembered instructions came to him – 'the same string over both times' – or 'under,' wasn't it?

Stephen crouched at his side, dazedly watching his mobile fingers muddling with the cord.

A step sounded outside on the pavement. Stephen woke up with a whispered 'My God!' and panic snatched at the pair of them. Feverishly John finished his knot and tugged at the ends. It was a 'granny,' he saw, but a granny it must remain. The steps had surely stopped outside the door.

'Quick,' he whispered, and got his right arm under the sack. Stumbling and straining, with a reckless disturbance of rugs and mats, they bundled the sagging body of Emily Gaunt into the dining-room. In the dining-room John Egerton halted and laid his end of her down. He was not strong, and she was heavy. Stephen clung to her feet, and the two of them stood listening, very shaky and afraid. There was no sound in the street now. The steps must have passed the door. From the rear there was the melancholy hooting of a tug, calling for its waiting barges at Ginger Wharf. They could hear the slow, methodical panting of her engines and the furtive swish of the water at her bows. In the garden a cat was wailing – horribly like a child in pain. To John Egerton these familiar sounds seemed like the noises of a new world, the new world he had entered at about a quarter-past nine, when he had become a partner, an accomplice, in this wretched piece of brutality and deceit. He felt curiously identified with it now – he was part of it, not merely an impersonal observer. He had a sensation of personal guilt.

'It's all right,' said somebody, very far away, in the voice of Stephen Byrne – a hoarse and furtive voice.

John Egerton picked up his burden, and another staggering stage was accomplished into the conservatory.

It was dusk now, but a large moon was up, and thin streams of silver filtered through the opaque roof and the crowded vine-leaves on to the long bundle on the floor. It was too light, Stephen thought, for this kind of work.

When they had halted he said, 'Wait a minute, John – I'll go and see if the coast is clear.' He went quickly down the stone steps into the tiny garden. The long, rich grass of Stephen's 'lawn' was drenched and glistening with dew. There was the heavy scent of something in the next-door garden, and over all a hot, intolerable stillness. Stephen became suddenly oppressed with the sense of guilt. Instinctively he stepped on to the wet grass and rustled softly through it to the river, his silk socks sponging up the dew.

Over the shallow wall he inspected furtively the silent river. Nothing moved. It was slack water, and the downward procession of tugs had not properly begun. The water was smooth; the black reflections of the opposite trees were sharp and perfect. Down towards Hammersmith a few lights hung like pendant jewels in the water. Over the far houses there was a flicker like summer lightning from an electric train. A huddle of driftwood and odd refuse floated motionless in mid-stream, very black and visible, waiting for the tide to turn; but along the edges the stream already crept stealthily down, lapping softly against the moored ranks of boats, against Stephen's boat riding comfortably beneath him. In the neighbouring gardens nothing moved. About this hour in the hot weather the residents of Hammerton Chase would creep out secretly into their gardens and cast their refuse into the river, and there was often to be heard at dusk a scattered succession of subdued splashes.

But tonight there was no splashes. Probably the duty was already done. Stephen remembered incongruously this local habit, and was at once relieved and disappointed. Too many people prowling in their gardens might be dangerous. On the other hand, there was a certain safety in a multitude of splashes. One more would have made no difference.

There were no splashes now, and scarcely any sound: only the fretful muttering of distant traffic, the occasional rumble of buses on the far-off bridge, and the small plops of fishes leaping at the moon. Close to Stephen was an unobtrusive munching in the wired space where Joan's rabbits were kept. A buck rabbit lay hunched in the moonlight masticating contentedly the last remnants of the evening cabbage. Another nosed at the wire-netting, begging without conviction for further illicit supplies. Stephen stooped down automatically and rubbed his nose.

But for the moonlight and the present

61

slackness of the tide the moment was propitious. Stephen walked back more boldly into the conservatory. 'You take the feet,' he said.

Without further speech they picked up the bundle and descended laboriously into the garden. The bright moon intimidated John. He looked back over his shoulder for people peering out of windows. But only the windows of his own house commanded the garden; and Mrs Bantam, his housekeeper, would be long since in bed. Paddling quietly through the dew, he, too, thought fantastically of other burdens he had smuggled down to the river on many a breathless night, pailfuls of potato-peelings and old tins and ashes. In his mind he gave a mute hysterical chuckle at the thought. What other residents, he wondered, had taken this kind of contraband through their gardens in the secret night? Old Dimple, the barrister – ha! ha! – or Mrs Ambrose? Perhaps they, too, had strangled people in their houses and consigned them guiltily to the condoning Thames. Perhaps all those sober, respectable people were capable, like Stephen, of astonishing crimes. Nothing, now, could be really surprising. God, what's that?

There was a sudden scuffle and clatter in the dark angle by the river wall – only the rabbits panicking into corners at the silent coming of a stranger. But John was aware of the violent beating of his heart.

They laid Emily on the ground and looked over the wall. The tide had now definitely turned. The middle stream was smoothly moving, oily and swift. John felt happier. It would soon be over now. An easy thing, to slip her over into the friendly water ... no more of this hideous heaving and fumbling with a cold body in a sweat of anxiety.

But to Stephen, regarding doubtfully the close row of boats a hundred yards downstream, new and disquieting uncertainties had occurred. To him, too, it had seemed a simple thing to drop Emily over the wall and let the river dispose of her. But supposing the river failed, flung her against the mooring-chain of one of those boats, jammed her with the tide under the sloping bows of Mr Adamson's decrepit hulk, left her there till the tide went down... He saw with a frightening clearness Emily Gaunt being discovered in the morning on the muddy foreshore of Hammerton Terrace – discovered by Andrews, the longshoreman, or a couple of small boys, or Thingummy Rawlins, prowling down from his garden to tinker with his motor-boat... No, that would never do.

He said in a low voice, 'John ... we'll have to take her out in the boat ... we can't just drop her... These damned boats ... supposing she caught...'

John Egerton uttered a long groan of

disappointment. It was not all over, then. There must be more liftings and irritations, more damnable association with this vileness.

'*O Lord!*' he protested. 'Stephen, I can't...' His face was pale and almost piteous under the moon.

Stephen answered him without petulance this time. 'John, old man – for God's sake, see it through ... we *must* get on, and I can't do it without you ... I'm awfully sorry ... it's got to be done...' The appeal in his voice succeeded as an irritable outburst could not have done.

John Egerton braced himself again. In his own mind he recognized the practical wisdom of using the boat. He said with a great weariness, 'Come on then.'

It was a long and difficult business getting that body into the boat. A flight of wooden steps led down from the wall to the water, and from there the boat – a small motor-boat, half-dinghy, half-canoe – had to be hauled in with a boathook for Stephen to step acrobatically into her and unfasten the moorings. Then she had to be paddled close up under the wall and fastened lightly to the steps. While Stephen was doing this a tug swished by, with a black string of barges clinging clumsily astern. The red eye of her port light glared banefully across the water. John felt that the man in that tug must guess infallibly what work he was at. A solitary lantern in the stern of the sternmost barge flickered about the single figure standing at the tiller. He could see the face of the man, turned unmistakably towards him.

She was travelling fast, and Stephen cursed as her wash took hold of his little boat and tossed her up and banged her against the wall and the rickety steps. John, leaning anxiously over, could hear his muttered execrations as he fended her off.

Then there was a hot, whispered argument – on the best way of getting the body down, Stephen standing swaying in the boat, with his face upturned, like some ridiculous moonlight lover, John flinging down assertions and reasonings in a forced whisper which broke now and then into a harsh undertone. Stephen thought it should be carted down the steps. John, with an aching objection to further prolonged contact with the thing, said it should be lowered with a rope. 'Haven't you a bit of rope?' he reiterated – 'a bit of rope – much the best.'

Sick of argument, Stephen fumbled with wild mutterings in his locker, and brought out in a muddle of oil-cans and tools a length of stout cord. Together they made a rough bight about Emily's middle, together lifted her to the flat stone parapet of the wall.

When she was there a dog barked suspiciously in Hammerton Terrace; another echoed him along The Chase. The two men crouched against the wall in a tense and

65

ridiculous agitation.

Through all these emergencies and arguments and muffled objurgations there stirred in John's mind ironical recollections of passages in detective stories, where dead bodies were constantly being transported with facility and dispatch in any desired direction. It seemed so easy in the books, it was so damnably difficult in practice – or so they were finding it.

And always there was the menace of Margery's return; she must be back soon, she would certainly come out into the garden on a night like this...

When they had the body stretched flat and ready on the wall, Stephen went back into the boat. It had sidled down below the steps, and had to be hauled back. The tide was maddeningly strong. Stephen urged the boat with imprecations under the wall. To keep it there he must hold on stoutly with a boat-hook, and could give little help to John in the detested task of lowering the sack. John's hands were clammy with sweat like the hands of a gross man. He gripped the rope with a desperate energy and thrust Emily gently over the side. The rope dragged and scraped across the parapet; the body swayed in the moonlight with a preposterous see-saw motion. When it was half-way to the water, they heard a tug puffing rhythmically towards them – somewhere beyond the

Island. It was not yet in sight, but a resistless unreasoning panic immediately invaded them. Stephen, with one free hand, clawed recklessly at an edge of sacking; John, in a furious effort to quicken the descent of Emily, lost altogether his control of the rope. The rope slipped swiftly through his moist and impotent palms. Emily, with an intimidating bump and a wooden clatter of sculls, fell ponderously into the boat and lay sprawled across the gunwale. A sibilant 'Damned fool!' slid up the wall from Stephen, almost overbalanced by the sudden descent of the body. The two men waited with an elaborate assumption of innocence while the tug fussed past, their hearts pounding absurdly. Then, before the wash had come, John Egerton stepped gingerly down the creaking steps, and they pushed out into the rolling reflection of the moon. The nose of the boat lifted, steeply on the oily swell of the tug's wash, and the head of Emily slipped down with a thump over the thwart, her feet still projecting obliquely over the side; John Egerton pulled them in. He looked back with a new disquiet at the still and silvery houses of Hammerton Terrace, at the dim shrubberies along The Chase. There were lights in some of the houses. Out there under the public moon he felt very visible and suspect – a naked feeling.

He heard a remote mutter from Stephen,

paddling in the bows: 'Too many of these damned tugs!' and another; 'This filthy *moon!*' They were working slowly against the tide between the Island and the mainland of The Chase. Stephen's plan was to round the top of the Island, cross the river, and get rid of Emily in the shadows of the other side, drifting down with the tide.

Even in the narrow channel by the bank the tide was exasperating, and paddling the boat, heavy with the engine, was slow work and strenuous. But the engine would be too noisy. And it was an uncertain starter.

Stephen said at last, 'Hell! get out of the sculls!'

John Egerton groped in the locker for rowlocks with an oppressive sense of incompetence and delay. His fingers moved with an ineffectual urgency in a messy confusion of spanners and oil-cans, tins of grease, and slimy labyrinths of thin cord. Only one rowlock was discoverable. The finding of the second became in his mind a task of inconceivable importance and difficulty. Vast issues depended on it – Stephen ... Margery ... babies ... Emily Gaunt ... and somehow or other Mrs Bantam. Thunderous mutterings rolled down distantly from the bows. John groaned helplessly. He caught his fingers sharply on the edge of a screw-driver... 'It's not here ... it's not here ... it *can't* be, Stephen.' With a sense of heroic measures he hauled out in clattering handfuls the whole muddle of implements in the locker. Under the electric coil lurked the missing rowlock.

'Row, then, like the devil,' ordered Stephen. Out here, in this strange watery adventure, Stephen was the readily acknowledged commander. John rowed, with grunts and splashings.

They rounded the Island, the moon glowing remotely beyond it through the traceries of young willow stems. Stephen was doing something with an anchor at the mouth of the sack, breathing audibly through his nose. John sculled obliquely across the river, struggling against the tide, steadily losing ground, he felt. 'Losing ground,' he thought insanely, 'ought to be losing *water*, of course.' So strangely do the minds of men move in critical hours.

When they were half-way over, the chunk-chunk of a motorboat came lazily upstream. 'God!' said Stephen, 'a police-boat.' John thought, 'Will it never end?' It was appalling, this accumulation of obstacles and delays and potential witness. He was tired now, and acutely conscious of a general perspiration.

They drifted downstream under the bank, while the police-boat phutted up on the far side, a low black shape without lights. Caped figures chattered easily in the stern and took no evident notice of the small white motor-boat under the bank; but Stephen and John imagined fatal suspicions and perceptions proceeding under the peaked caps. They passed.

'*Now!*' Stephen was fiddling with his anchor again, tugging at a knot; his tone was final. 'Take her out into the middle again … *quick!*'

John pulled gallantly with his left. They were opposite the house again now, moving smoothly towards Hammersmith Bridge. No other craft was in sight or sound.

Stephen said thickly, 'If we don't get her over now, we never shall … stand by… No, no … you trim the boat… I'll manage it…'

He edged Emily close up against the gunwale, her extremities on a couple of thwarts, her middle sagging down the side of the boat. He looked quickly up the river and down the river and at Hammerton Terrace and at the oilmills below and at the empty tow-path on the opposite bank, all silent, all still. Stephen put a hand under the sack. Close by a tiny fish leaped lightly from the river. Stephen saw the flash of its belly, and took his hand away with a start. Then with a great heave under Emily's middle, a violent pushing and lifting with feet and body and arms, that set the sculls clattering and the boat precariously rocking, he got the body half over the gunwale, John, perched anxiously on the other side, striving to correct the already dangerous list. Stephen struggled blasphemously with the infuriating sack. Somehow, somewhere it was maddeningly entangled with something in the boat. Frantic tugging and thrusting, irritable oaths, moved it not at all. John looked fearfully behind him. A lighted omnibus was swimming through space, perilously near ... Hammersmith Bridge. Stephen was kicking the body now with a futile savagery.

'What the hell?' he said. 'O God!'

John groped distantly with a hand in the dark. Then, 'The anchor!' he said – 'the anchor's caught...' He heard a relieved 'O Lord!' from Stephen, 'thought I'd put the anchor end over first' – and for the first time made himself a petulant comment, 'Why the devil didn't you?' It was too much – this sort of thing. Then the shaggy end of the sack was slithering quietly over the side, the anchor twinkled swiftly in the moon, and the relieved boat rocked suddenly with a wild, delighted levity. Emily was gone.

Peering back upstream, the two men saw a slowly expanding circle on the black water. And there were a few bubbles. Emily was indeed gone.

Stephen sat in a limp posture of absolute exhaustion, his shoulders hunched, his head on his hands, speechless.

John looked at his watch. It was a quarter-past ten – only about an hour since Emily

71

died. He stared incredulous at the faintly luminous bands. Then he looked round; the boat seemed to be drifting very fast. On his right were the boathouses, a dark huddle of boats clinging to the rafts in front of them. The boathouses were next to the Bridge.

He looked back and up, with a new fear. The long span of the suspension bridge hung almost above them. A bus rumbled ominously above. Two persons were standing on the footpath against the parapet, looking down at the boat. He could see the pale blobs of their faces. One of them had a Panama hat.

The boat shot into the dark under the Bridge.

John leaned forward. 'Stephen,' he whispered – 'Stephen.' There was no answer. John touched his knee. 'Stephen.'

A yellow face lifted slowly. 'What is it?'

'There was someone watching on the Bridge ... two men.'

Stephen sighed with a profound weariness. 'It can't be helped,' he said.

A dreadful paralysis seemed to have succeeded the heavy strain. He looked as men used to look after a long spell in the line, sitting at last in a dingy billet – played out.

John Egerton took the sculls and turned the boat round. The boat moved stiffly, with a steady gurgle at the bows; the noiseless tide swung violently by; the oars creaked complainingly.

'This *tide*...' muttered John.

Stephen Byrne raised his head. 'The tide's going out,' he said stupidly.

CHAPTER IV

Margery Byrne walked home very happily from the Underground Station at Stamford Brook. The ticket collector uttered a reverent 'Good night, mum'; the policeman at the corner of St Peter's Square brightened suddenly at her and saluted with the imperishable manner of past military service. The world was very kind and friendly, she felt. But that was the usual manner of the world to Margery Byrne. The world invariably looked at her as it passed her in the street. The male world invariably looked again. The mannerless male world usually looked back. The shameless male world stared at her in Tubes and manoeuvred obviously for commanding positions. But that part of the world, having secured its positions, was generally either disappointed or abashed. There was an aspect of fragility and virtue about her which stirred in the bold and shameless male the almost atrophied instincts of chivalry and protection. After a little they ceased to stare, but opened doors for her with a conscious knighthood. There are women who make a man feel evil at the sight of them. Margery made a man feel good.

But this aspect of fragility was without any suggestion of feebleness. It was just that she was slight and fair, and her face small and her features intensely delicate and refined. She had a rarefied look – as if all flaws and imperfections and superfluities had been somehow chemically removed, leaving only the essential stamina and grace. For she had stamina. She walked with an easy un-urban swing, and she could walk a long way. Her lips were little and slightly anaemic, but firm. There was an evident will in the determined and perfectly proportioned chin. The nose was small but admirably straight and set very close above the mouth. Only her large blue eyes seemed a little out of proportion, but these suggested a warm sympathy which the smallness of her features might otherwise have concealed. Her head, balanced attract-ively on straight white shoulders, was covered gloriously, if a little thinly, with hair of a light gold, an indescribable tint not often encountered outside the world of books. But such, in fact, was Margery's hair. Her skin also was of a colour and texture not to be painted in words – it had that indefinable quality for which there has been discovered no better name than transparent. And this pale, almost colourless quality of complexion completed the effect of fragility, of physical refinement.

It was still and sultry in St Peter's Square. The old moon hung above the church and lit up the ridiculous stone eagles on the decayed and pompous houses on Margery's right. 'Like lecterns,' she thought, for the thousandth time.

The houses were square and semi-detached, two in one; a life-size eagle perched over every porch, its neck screwed tragically towards its sister-eagle craning sympathetic-ally on the neighbouring porch, seeking apparently for ever a never-to-be-attained communion. What sort of people lived there, Margery wondered, and why? So far from town and no view of the river, no special attraction. The people of The Chase always wondered in this way as they walked through St Peter's Square. The problems of who lived in it and why were permanently insoluble – since nobody who lived in The Chase knew anybody who lived in the Square. They knew each other, and that was enough. They knew it was worth while travelling a long way if you lived in The Chase, because of the river, the views, the openness, and the fine old rambling, rickety houses. But why should anyone live in an inland square with eagles over the front doors?

Margery did not know. And she had other things to think of. Tomorrow she must speak seriously to Emily. Emily, like all these young women, had started excellently, but was becoming slack. And impertinent, sometimes. But one must be careful. Just now was not the time to frighten her away. Then Trueman's man was coming for the curtains in the morning; they must be got ready. And there was a mountain of needlework to be done. And she must run through Stephen's clothes again – before she was too ill for it. Only a month more now, perhaps less. That was a blessing. She was not frightened this time – not like the first time, with little Joan – that *had* been rather terrifying – not knowing quite what it was like. But it was a long, interminable business; for such ages, it seemed, you had to 'be careful,' not play tennis, or go out to dinner just when you wanted to. You felt a fool sometimes, inventing reasons for not doing things, when of course there was only one reason. And so ugly – especially in London ... going about in shops ... and Tubes.

Never mind. It was worth it. And afterwards...

Margery cast her mind deliciously forward to that 'afterwards.' They would all go away somewhere, her dear Stephen and Joan and a new and adorable little Stephen. She was determined that it should be a boy this time.

That was what Stephen wanted, and what he wanted, within reason, he should have. He deserved it, the dear man. Really, he was becoming an amazingly perfect husband. Becoming, yes – for just at first he had been difficult. But that was during the war; they had seen so little of each other – and he was always worried, overworked. But now they had really 'settled down,' the horrid war was done with, and he had been too wonderfully delightful and nice to her. Lately especially. Much more considerate and helpful and – and, yes, demonstrative. She felt more sure of him. She was appalled, sometimes, to think how essential he was to her, how frightfully dependent she had become on the existence of this one man, met quite by chance, or what was called chance, at somebody else's house. If anything should happen now– Even the children would be a poor consolation.

But nothing would happen. He would go on being more and more delicious and successful; she would go on being happy and proud, watching eagerly the maturement of her ambitions for him. Even now she was intensely proud of him – though, of course, it would never do to let him suspect it.

It was an astounding thing, this literary triumph. Secretly, she admitted, she had never had enormous faith in his poetical powers. She had liked his work because it was his. And being the daughter of a mildly literary man, she had developed a serious critical faculty capable of generously appraising any artistic effort of real sincerity and promise. But she had seldom thought of Stephen's poetry in terms of the market, of public favour and material reward. Certainly she had not married him as 'a poet' or even 'a writer.' But that only made his meteoric success more dazzling and delightful. Sometimes it was almost impossible to realize, she found, that this young man she had married was the same Stephen Byrne whose name was everywhere – on the bookstalls, in the publishers' advertisements, in literary articles in any paper you picked up; that all over the country men and women were buying and reading and re-reading and quoting and discussing bits of poetry which *her* husband had scribbled down on odd bits of paper at her own house. It was astounding. Margery was passing the small houses at the end of the Square, the homes of clerks and shop-people and superior artisans. She glanced at a group of wives, garrulously taking the air at a doorway, and almost pitied them because *their* husbands' names were never before the public. It sounded awful, now, to be absolutely obscure.

No. She didn't think that really. After all, it was an 'extra', this fame. It had nothing to do with her marrying Stephen; it would have nothing to do with her happiness with

Stephen. It was a kind of matrimonial wind-fall. 'What really mattered was Stephen himself, and Margery herself, and the way in which they fitted together. What she really – yes, *adored* – there was no other word – was himself, his black hair and his twinkling smile, his laugh and jolliness and funny little ways. And his character. That, of course, was the foundation of it all. A dear and excellent character. Other men, even the best of them, did horrid things sometimes. Stephen, she knew, with all his faults – a little selfish, perhaps – conceited? no, but self-centred, rather – would never do anything mean or degrading or treacherous. She could trust him absolutely. He would certainly never disgrace her as some men did disgrace their wives – women, drink, and so on. 'The soul of honour' – that was the phrase... That, again, was a marvellous piece of fortune, that out of a world of peccant questionable men she should have been allowed to appro-priate a man like Stephen, so nearly perfect and secure. No wonder she had this con-suming, this frightening sense of adoration, sometimes. But she tried to suppress that. It was dangerous. 'Thou shalt not bow down...'

Margery smiled secretly and turned her latch-key in the lock.

In the hall she noticed immediately Stephen's hat on the peg, and was glad that he was home. She walked through with her letters to the garden, and looked out over the wall. The boat was gone, and she was faintly disappointed. Far down the river she fancied she saw it, a dirty whiteness, and resisted an impulse to call to Stephen. It must be nice on the river tonight. The rabbits rustled stealthily in the corner; a faint unpleasant smell hung about their home. She looked absently at the rabbit Paul, his nose twitching endlessly in the moonlight, and went in to bed.

When she had undressed she leaned for a long time out of the high window looking at the night. Across the river lay the broad reservoirs of the water company, and the first houses were half a mile away; so that from the window on a night like this you looked over seemingly endless stretches of gleaming water; strangers coming there at night-time wondered at the wide spaciousness of this obscure corner of London. You could imagine yourself easily in some Oriental city. Hammersmith and Chiswick and Barnes wore a romantic coat of shadow and silver. The carved reflections of the small trees on the other bank were so nearly like reflected rows of palms. The far-off outline of factories against the sky had all the awe and mystery of mosques. In the remote murmur of London traffic there was the note, at once lazy and sinister, treacherous and reposeful, of an Eastern town. And now when no tugs went by and nothing stirred, the silent river, rushing smoothly into the black heart of London, had for Margery something of the sombre majesty of the Nile, hinting at dark unnameable things, passion and death and furtive cruelties, and all that sense of secrecy and crime which clings to the river-side of great cities, the world over.

Margery wondered idly how much of all that talk about the Thames was true; whether horrible things were still done secretly beside her beloved river, hidden and condoned by the river, carried away to the sea... Down in the docks, no doubt... Wapping and so on.

The prosaic thumping of a tug broke the spell of Margery's imagination. She looked up and down for Stephen's boat, a faint crossness in her mind because of his lateness. She got into bed. She was sleepy, but she would read and doze a little till he came in.

She woke first drowsily to the hollow sound of oars clattering in a boat, a murmur of low voices and subdued splashings ... Stephen mooring the boat ... how late he was.

A long while afterwards, it seemed, she woke again: Stephen was creaking cautiously up the stairs. She felt that he was peeping at her round the door, murmured sleepily, 'How late you are,' dimly comprehended his soft excuses ... something about the tide ... caught by the tide ... engine went wrong ...

of course ... always did ... raised her head with a vast effort to be kissed a very delicate and reverent kiss ... remembered to ask if Cook was back ... mustn't lock the front door ... half heard a deep 'Good night, my darling, go to sleep' and drifted luxuriously to sleep again, to comfortable dreams of Stephen, dreams of babies ... moonlight ... special editions ... palm trees and water – peaceful, silvery water.

Long afterwards there was a distant fretful interruption, hardly heeded. A stir outside. Cook's voice ... Stephen's voice ... something about Emily. Emily Gaunt ... not come home ... must speak seriously to Emily tomorrow ... can't be bothered now. Stephen see to it ... Stephen and Cook. Cook's voice, raucous. Cook's night out ... late ... go to bed, Cook ... go to bed ... go to bed, everybody ... all's well.

Stephen turned out the light and crept away to the little room behind, thanking God for the fortunate sleepiness of his wife. The dreaded moment had passed.

He sat down wearily on the bed and tried to reduce the whirling tangle in his brain to order. He ought, of course, to be thinking things out, planning precautions, explanations, studied ignorances. But he was too muddled, too tired. God, how tired! Lugging that hateful sack about. And that awful row home – more than a mile against the tide, though John had done most of that, good old John... (There was something disturbing he had said to John, when they parted at last – what the devil was it? ... something had slipped out... An intangible, uneasy memory prodded him somewhere ... no matter.) And then when he did get back, what a time he had had in the scullery, tidying the refuse on the floor, groping about under a table ... hundreds of pieces of paper, grease-paper, newspaper, paper bags, orange skins, old tins, bottles... He had gathered them all and put them in a bucket, a greasy bucket, with tea-leaves at the bottom ... carried it down to the river on tiptoe ... four journeys. God, what a night!

But it was over now – it was all over – that part of it. All that was wanted now was a straight face, a little acting, and some straightforward lying. 'God knows, I can lie all right,' Stephen thought, 'though nobody knows it.' What lie was it he had invented about the sack, tired as he was? Oh yes, that John had borrowed it, and that John had first emptied the rubbish into the river... Yes, he had coached John on the steps about that ... told him to keep it up if necessary. Old John had looked funny when he said that. John didn't like lies, even necessary ones. A bit of a prig, old John.

Stephen pulled at the bow of his black tie and fumbled at the stud. He took off one sock and scratched his ankle reflectively. It was a pity about John. He was such a good fellow, really, such a good friend. He had helped splendidly tonight, invaluable. But God knew what he felt about it all... Shocked, of course... Flabbergasted (whatever that meant). The question was, how would he get over the shock? How would he feel when he woke up? Would he be permanently shocked, stop being friends?... He was a friend worth keeping, old John. And his opinion was worth having, his respect. Anyhow, it was going to be awkward. One would always feel a bit mean and ashamed now with John – in the wrong, somehow... Stephen hated to feel in the wrong.

Cook lumbered breathlessly up the stairs, and halted with a loud sigh on the landing. She knocked delicately on Mrs Byrne's door and threw out a tentative, 'If you please, mum.' Stephen went out. The acting must begin.

'What is it, Mrs Beach – speak low – Mrs Byrne's asleep.'

'It's Emily, sir, if you please, sir, turned half-past eleven now, sir, and she's not in the house. I didn't speak before, sir, thinking she might have slipped out like for a bit of a turn and met a friend like. She weren't in the kitchen, sir, when I come in, nor in the bedroom neither. I thought perhaps as how you'd seen her, sir, when you come in and sent her on a herrand like. What had I best do sir shall I lock up sir it's late for a young girl and gone out without her mack too.'

Mrs Beach concluded her remarks with a long, unpunctuated peroration as if fearful that her scanty wind should fail altogether before she had fully delivered herself.

Stephen thought rapidly. Had he sent Emily out on a 'herrand,' or had he not seen her at all?

He said, 'No, Mrs Beach, I didn't see her; I went straight out on to the river. No doubt she went out for a little walk and met a friend, as you say. She'll be back soon, no doubt, and I'm afraid you'll have to let her in ... very naughty of her to stay out so late. Nothing to be done, I fear. Good night, Mrs Beach.'

Mrs Beach caught sympathetically at Stephen's meaning suggestion of Emily's naughtiness. 'Good night, sir,' she puffed; 'she always was a one for the young men, though I says it myself, but there youth will 'ave its fling, they say, and sorry I am to disturb you, sir, but I thought as I'd best speak, it was that late, sir.'

'Quite right, Mrs Beach. Good night.'

'Good night, sir.'

Mrs Beach sighed herself ponderously down the dark stairs. Stephen went back into his room with a startling sense of elation. He had done that well. It would be marvellously easy if it was all like that. That word 'naughty' had been a masterpiece; he was proud of it. Already he had set moving a plausible explanation of Emily's disappearance – Emily's frailty – Emily's 'friend.' Cook would do the rest. Mentally he chuckled.

Suddenly then he appreciated the vileness on which he was congratulating himself, and the earlier blackness settled upon him. Something like conscience, something like remorse, had room to stir in place of his abated fears. It was going to be a wretched business, this 'easy' lying and hypocrisy and deceit – endless stretches of wickedness seemed to open out before him. What a mess it was! How the devil had it happened – to him, Stephen Byrne, the reputed, respectable young author?

Suddenly – like the lights fusing... What, in Heaven's name, had made him do it? Emily Gaunt, of all people... Curse Emily! He wasted no pity on her, no sentimental sorrow for the wiping out of a warm young life. Emily had brought it on herself, the little fool. It was her fault – really... Stephen was too self-centred to be gravely disturbed by thoughts of Emily, except so far as she was likely to affect his future peace of mind. And he had seen too much of death in the war to be much distressed by the fact of death. His inchoate remorse was more of a protest than a genuine regret for wrong – a protest against the wounding of his self-respect, against the coming worries and anxieties and necessary evasions, and all the foreseen unpleasantness which this damnable night had forced upon him. It must not happen again, this kind of thing. Too upsetting. Stephen began to make fierce resolutions, as sincere as any resolutions can be that rest on such unsubstantial foundations. He was going to be a better fellow in future – a better husband... People thought a lot of him at present – and they were deceived. In future he would live up grandly to 'people's' conception of him, to Margery's conception of him.

When he thought of Margery he was suddenly and intensely ashamed. That aspect of his conduct he had so far managed to ignore. Now he became suddenly hot at the thought of it. He had behaved damnably to Margery. Supposing she had come back earlier, discovered Emily. 'A – a – ah!' A strangled exclamation burst from him, as men groan in spite of themselves at some story of brutality or pain. Sweat stood about his temples. Poor Margery, so patient and loving and trustful. What a swine he had been! The resolutions swelled enormously ... no more drinking ... the drink had done it ... he would knock it off altogether. No, not altogether – that was silly, unnecessary. In moderation. He slipped his trousers to the floor.

Margery thought too much of him, believed in him too well. It was terrible, in a way, being an idol; life would be easier if one had a bad reputation, even an ordinary 'man-of-the-world' reputation. A character of moral perfection was a heavy burden, if you were not genuinely equal to it. Never mind, in future, he *would* be equal to it; he *would* be perfect. Tender and chivalrous thoughts of Margery invaded him; the resolutions surged wildly up, an almost religious emotion glowed warmly inside him; he felt somehow as he used to feel at Communion, walking back to his seat. He used to pray in those days, properly... He felt like praying now.

He tied the string of his pyjamas and knelt down by the small bed. It was a long time since he had prayed. During the war, in tight corners, when he had been terribly afraid, he had prayed the sick, emergency supplications of all soldiers – the 'O God, get me out of this and I will be good' kind of prayer. The *padres* used to preach sermons about such prayers, and sometimes Stephen had determined to pray always, at the safe times as well as the dangerous, but this had never lasted for long. Now his prayers were on the same note, wrung out of him like his resolutions by the urgent emotions of the moment, sincere but bodiless.

He prayed, 'O God, I have been a fool and a swine. O God, forgive me for this night's work and get me out of the mess safely, and I will – I will be good.' That was the only way of expressing it – 'being good,' like a child. 'In future I will be a better man and pray more often. O God, keep this from Margery, for her sake, not mine. O God, forgive me, and make me better. Amen.'

Stephen rose from his knees, a little relieved, but with an uncomfortable sense of bargaining. It was difficult to pray without driving a bargain, somehow ... like some of those wretched hymns:

> *'And when I see Thee as Thou art*
> *I'll praise Thee as I ought,'*

for instance, a close, inescapable contract. The old tune sang in his head. But if one prayed properly, no doubt one learned to exclude that commercial flavour– How hot it was!

He turned out the lights and crept slowly under the sheets. For a long time he lay staring at the dark, thinking now of Emily's night-dress... Probably it was marked – in neat red letters – Emily Gaunt. Probably the sacking would wear away where the rope went through it, dragging with the tide. Probably... Hideous possibilities crowded back and gloom returned to him. And what

89

was it he had said to John? He had forgotten about that. Something silly had slipped out, when John had looked so shocked, something intended to soothe John's terrible conscience, something about 'doing the right thing afterwards' – after the baby had safely come. 'I'll put things right then,' he remembered saying. What the devil had he meant by that? What did John think he had meant? Hell!

Stephen threw off the blanket; he was sweating again.

When the cold chime of St Peter's struck three he lay still maddeningly awake in a feverish muddle of thought. Then at last he slept, dreaming wildly.

Emily Gaunt shifted uneasily in her oozy bed, tugging at her anchor, as the tide rolled down.

CHAPTER V

Every misfortune which can happen to a man who travels Underground in London had happened to John Egerton. Worn and irritable with a sultry day at the Ministry he had jostled with a shuffling multitude on to the airless platform at Charing Cross. From near the bottom of the stairs he saw that an

Ealing train was already in; more important, the train was stopping at Stamford Brook. Stamford Brook was a 'non-stop station,' so that if you missed your train in the busy hours you might wait for an intolerable time. On this sweltering evening it was urgent to escape as quickly as possible from the maddening crowd of sticky citizens and simpering girls. It was urgent to catch that train. Already they were slamming home the doors. John made a nightmare attempt to hurry down the last few steps and across to that train. His way was blocked by a mob of deliberate backs, unaccountably indifferent to the departure of the Ealing train, and moving with exasperating slowness. John, with mumbled and insincere apologies, dived through the narrow alley between a portly man and a portly woman. Whistles were blowing now, but once down the stairs the way would be fairly clear to the desirable train. Only round the foot of the stairs hovered a bewildered family, a shoal of small children clinging to their expansive mother and meagre sire, wondering stupidly what they ought to do next in this strange muddle of a place. They were back from some country jaunt and bristled with mackintoshes and small chairs and parcels and spades and other impassable excrescences.

John governed himself and said, 'Excuse me, please,' with a difficult assumption of calm. None of them moved. John longed to seize the little idiots by the throat and fling them aside, to knock down the meagre man and trample upon him. Instead, he shouted aggressively, 'Let me pass, please!' – the train was moving now. The large woman looked back, with a frightened air, shot out an arm with a sharp 'Mabel!' and plucked her first-born daughter aside by the flesh of her arm pinched painfully between finger and thumb. The child screeched, but the way was clear, and John flung forward. An open door was moving almost opposite to him; he had only to swing himself in. Then from nowhere appeared a youthful uniformed official, who barred the way with an infuriating aspect of authority, and slammed fast the receding door. The train slid clattering past and vanished with a parting flicker of blue flashes. The boy walked off with an Olympian and incorruptible air, not looking at John, as who should say, 'Tamper not with me.' Interfering ass! John had an impulse to go after and abuse him, demonstrate with fierce argument the folly of the youth. The waiting crowd observed him with the heartless amusement of crowds, hoping secretly that he would lose his temper, provide entertainment. John saw them and controlled himself, thinking with a conscientious effort, 'His duty, I suppose,' and contented himself with a long glower at the obstructive family.

The next train was a Wimbledon one; the next an Inner Circle; the next a Richmond, not stopping at Stamford Brook. The endless people shuffled always down the stairs, drifted aimlessly along the platform, jostled and barged good-humouredly about the teeming trains. Government flappers congregated giggling in small groups, furtively examined by ambulant young men. In spite of the heat and the stuffy smell of humanity and the exasperation of crowded travelling there was a pleasant atmosphere of contentment and goodwill. Only here and there were the fretful and distressed, mainly country-folk, unaccustomed to the hardships of London. Tonight the equable John was among these petulant ones, which was unusual. He was worried and depressed – in no mood for a prolonged entanglement with a hot crowd. Never had he waited so long. Number 1 on the indicator now was a Putney train; Number 2 another Inner Circle – what the devil did they want with so many Circle trains? And why was Stamford Brook a non-stop station? Hundreds of people used it – far more than Sloane Square, for example, or St James's Park. He would write a letter to the Company about these things. The terms of his letter began to frame themselves in his mind – conceived in the best Civil Service style: 'It is evident ... convenience of greatest number of passengers ... revised programme

... facilities ... volume of traffic...' The Putney train racketed away; Number 2 was an Ealing now. John edged up to the glaring bookstall and stood with a row of men staring idly at the dusty covers of old sevenpennies – price two shillings. None of the men bought anything, only stood silent and gazed, as if in wonder, at such a multitude of unbuyable books. On the cover of one of them – *Three Years with the Hapsburgs: the Thrilling Chronicle of an English Governess* – the gaudy picture of a young woman caught his eye. It reminded him somehow of Emily Gaunt, and he turned away. He did not want to be reminded of Emily.

The Ealing train came in, and John was swept in with a tight mass of people through the middle doors of a smoking carriage. The atmosphere was a suffocating mixture of hot breath and evil tobacco-smoke. The carriage was packed. Men and women stood jammed together like troops in a communication-trench. Here and there a clerk stood up with a sheepish mumble and a sallow woman sank thankfully into his seat. John stared with increasing resentment at the rows of men who did not get up – tired labourers in corduroy trousers who sat on in unmoved contentment, or gross men with cigars who screened themselves behind evening papers, pretending they did not notice the standing women.

The train stopped, and there was a fierce squeezing and struggling at the doors. A man behind John remembered suddenly that he wanted to get out, and began with much heaving and imprecation to hew a passage, treading violently on John's ankle. But by now there were more people surging inwards, clinging precariously to the fringe of the mob. The train rushed on, and the man was left within it, cursing feebly. John felt glad, maliciously, ridiculously glad. But when he looked again at the sedentary gross men, the placid labourers, and at the short, pale women swaying in the centre, he became righteously furious with the evil manners of the men. He felt that he would like to address them, curse them about it – that fat one with the insolent leer and the cap all cock-eye, especially; he would say loudly at the next station, 'Why don't you give one of these ladies your seat?' Then the men would *have* to get up, would stand shamed before the world, while some grateful female – that nurse there – took his seat. Perhaps all the others would follow.

Or perhaps it would happen quite differently. The man would not hear, or pretend not to hear; and he, John, would have to repeat his remark, losing greatly in dramatic force. And every one would stare at him, as if he were a madman! Or the man would surrender his seat with a sweet smile and an apology, 'Very sorry, I didn't see'; and then the fools of women would refuse to take the seat. They would all say they were getting out at the next station; they would all simper and deprecate and behave like lunatics. The man would hover with a self-righteous, ingratiating smirk and sit down again. And John Egerton would look a fool. No – it couldn't be done. What cowards men were!

A very hot and spotty man breathed disgustingly in John's face; unable to move his body, he turned his head away to the left. On that side stood a robust young woman, with hatpins menacingly projecting from a red straw hat. Her head rocked as the train jolted: the cherries on her hat bobbed ridiculously, the naked hatpin-points swung backwards and forwards in front of John's eye. He turned back to the disgusting breath of the spotty man.

At Earl's Court the crowd melted a little; there were no seats, but there was room to breathe – room to stand by oneself, free from the pressure of strange bodies. At Baron's Court he crept into a seat. At Hammersmith a noisy mob of shop-girls and hobbledehoys surged in, and he surrendered his seat to a young woman, who was munching something. She sat down with a giggle and took her sister on her lap. Together they eyed him, with whispered jocularities. Only two more stations.

The lights were out now. The train ran out through the daylight on to a high embankment, past an interminable series of dingy houses. There was more air. The filthy smoke eddied out of the narrow windows. The train rocked enormously – a bad piece of line. Looking down the car from his place by the door, John saw through the haze an interminable vista of uniform right hands fiercely clinging to uniform straps, of right arms uniformly crooked, of bowed heads uniformly bent over evening papers, of endless backs uniformly enduring and dull. And as the train gave a great lurch, all the elbows swung out together towards the windows, and all the bodies bent outward like willows in the wind, and all the heads were lifted together in a mute and uniform protest. It was all like some fantastic physical drill. Then he fell into the weary stupor of the habitual Underground traveller, listening semi-consciously to the insane chatter of the chuckling girls. Ravenscourt Park shot by unnoticed. The train ran on for ever.

Stooping suddenly, he saw the familiar letters of Stamford Brook dashing past at an astonishing speed. Surely – surely the train was stopping. The porters' room – the ticket collector – the passenger-shelter – the Safety First pictures – the advertisement of What Ho! – the other name-board of the station – the whole station – shot maddeningly past.

The train rushed on to the intolerable remoteness of Turnham Green. Hell! John Egerton uttered an audible groan of vexation. *Two* non-stop trains running! It was unpardonable. He had not even thought to look at the non-stop labels on the train at Charing Cross. It was too bad. Another matter for the letter to the Company! The women looked at his scowling face and giggled again, whispering behind their hands.

From Turnham Green you might walk home; but it took nearly twenty minutes. Or if you were lucky you caught a train quickly back to Stamford Brook. As they came into the station, John saw an up-train gliding off on the other side of the same platform. Of course! just missed it! And no doubt the next one would decline to stop at Stamford Brook! Once you began having bad luck on the Underground you might as well give up all hope of improving it that day. You might as well walk. He *would* walk. But how damnable it all was!

He waited with the thick crowd at the ticket gate, fumbling for his ticket in his waistcoat pocket. That was where he had put it – he always did. Always in the same place – as a methodical man should do. But it was not there. It was not in the other waistcoat pocket – nor in his right-hand trouser pocket. 'Now, then,' said an aggressive voice behind, and he stepped aside. Lost his place in the queue, now! He put down his dispatch-case and felt furiously in his pockets with both hands. The passengers dwindled down the stairs; he was left alone, regarded indifferently by the bored official. This was the fitting climax to an abominable journey.

He found it at last, lurking in the flap of a tobacco pouch, and because he had come too far he was forced to pay another penny. There was a preposterous argument. 'Putting a premium on inconvenience!'

He walked home at last, cursing foolishly, and adding new periods to his letter to the Company. All over London men and women walked back to their homes that evening through the hot streets, bitter and irritated and physically distressed, ruminating on the problem of over-population and the difficulties of movement in the hub of the world – only a small proportion, it is true, as bitter and irritated as John, but every night the same proportion, every night a thousand or two. Historians, it is to be hoped, and scientists and statisticians, when they write up their estimates of that year, will not fail to record the mental and physical fatigue, the waste of tissue and nervous energy, imposed upon the citizens of our great Metropolis by the simple necessity of proceeding daily from their places of work to their places of residence. Small things, these irritations, an odd penny here, an odd ten minutes there, the difference between just catching and just missing a train, the difference between just standing for twenty minutes, and just sitting down – but they mounted up! They mounted up into vast excrescences of discourtesy and crossness; they made calm and equable and polite persons suddenly and amazingly abrupt and unkind.

John Egerton was seldom so seriously ruffled; but then it was seldom that so peculiarly unfortunate a journey concluded so peculiarly painful a day. A sticky and intolerable day. A 'rushed' and ineffectual day. 'Things' had shown a deliberate perversity at the office, papers had surprisingly lost themselves and thereafter surprisingly discovered themselves at the most awkward moments; telephone girls had been pert, telephone numbers permanently engaged. The Board of Trade had behaved execrably. John's own Minister had been unusually curt – jumpy.

And hovering at the back of it all, a kind of master irritation, which governed and stimulated every other one, was the unpleasant memory of Emily Gaunt.

So that he walked down the Square in a dark and melancholy temper. And Emily Gaunt met him on the doorstep. The skinny successor of Emily Gaunt in the household of the Byrnes stood at the doorway of his house, talking timidly to Mrs Bantam. She had come for 'some sack or other,' Mrs Bantam explained. 'And there's no sack in this house – that I *will* swear.' She spoke with the violent emphasis of all Mrs Bantams, as if the presence of a sack in a gentleman's house would have been an almost unspeakable offence against chastity and good taste. The skinny maid turned from her with relief to the less formidable presence of John.

'If you please, sir, Cook says as the missus says as Mrs Byrne says as – as' – the skinny maid faltered in this interminable forest of 'as's' – 'as you 'ad the big sack that was in the scullery, sir, and if you've done with it, sir, could we 'ave it back, sir, as the man's come for the bottles?'

The sack! Emily's sack! John had no need of the young woman's exposition. He remembered vividly. He remembered now what Stephen had said about it – in the boat – under the wall. John had 'borrowed' it. He remembered now. But what the devil had he borrowed it for? And why – why should he have to stand on his own doorstep this terrible day and invent lies for a couple of women?

And what had the man coming for the bottles to do with it, he wondered?

But a lie must be invented – and quickly. He said, 'Will you tell Mrs Byrne, I'm very sorry – I took the sack out in my boat – to –

to collect firewood – and – and – lost it – overboard, you know? Tell her I'm very sorry, will you, and I'll get her another sack?' He tried to smile nicely at the young woman; a painful smirk revealed itself.

'Thank you, sir.'

The young woman melted away, and he walked indoors, feeling sullied and ashamed. He hated telling lies. He was one of those uncommon members of the modern world who genuinely object to the small insincerities of daily life, lying excuses over the telephone for not going out to dinner, manufactured 'engagements,' and so on. And the fact that this lie was part of a grand conspiracy to protect a man from an indictment for murder did not commend it. On the contrary, it enhanced that feeling of 'identification' with the end of Emily which he had been trying for two weeks to shake off. Oh, it was damnable!

For his solitary dinner he opened a bottle of white wine – a rare indulgence. He hoped earnestly that Mrs Bantam would be less communicative than usual. Mrs Bantam had cooked and kept house for him for six months. She was one of that invaluable body of semi-decayed but capable middle-aged females who move through the world scorning and avoiding the company of their own sex, and seeking for single gentlemen with households; single gentlemen without female encumbrances; single gentlemen over whom they may exercise an undisputed dominion; single gentlemen who want 'looking after,' who are incapable of ordering their own food or 'seeing to' their clothes, who would, it is to be supposed, fade helplessly out of existence but for the constant comfort and support of their superior cook-housekeepers.

Mrs Bantam was intensely superior. From what far heights of luxury and distinction she had descended to the obscure kitchen of Island Lodge could be dimly apprehended from her dignity and her vocabulary and an occasional allusive passage in her conversation. She was as the transmigrant soul of some domestic pig, faintly aware of a nobler status in some previous existence. Where or what that existence had been John had never discovered; only he knew that it was noble, and that it had ended abruptly many years ago with the inconsiderate decease of 'my hubby'.

Mrs Bantam, for all her dignity, was scraggy, and had the aspect of chronic indigestion and decay. She was draped for ever in funereal black, partly in memory of hubby, partly, no doubt, because black was 'superior.' She walked, or rather proceeded, with an elegant stoop, her head stuck forward like an investigating hen, her long arms hanging straight down in front of her from her stooping shoulders like plumb-lines suspended from a leaning tower. Her face was pinched and marvellously pale, and her black eyes retreated into unfathomable recesses. Her chin receded and ended suddenly in a kind of fold, from which a flabby isthmus of skin went straight to the base of her throat, like the neck of a fowl; in this precarious envelope an Adam's apple of operatic dimensions moved up and down with alarming velocity.

Like so many of the world's greatest personalities, she had a noble soul, but she would make speeches. Her intercourse with others was one long oration. And she was too urbane. When she laid the bacon before her gentleman of the moment as he gazed moodily at his morning paper, she would ask pardon in a shrill chirp, like the notes of a superannuated yodeller, for 'passing in front' of him. This used to drive John as near to distraction as a Civil Servant can safely go. And though she had watched over him for six months, she still reminded him at every meal that she was as yet, of course, ill-acquainted with his tastes, and therefore unable to cater for those peculiar whims and fancies in which he differed from the last gentleman. By keeping sedulously alive this glorious myth she was able to disdain all responsibility for her choice and treatment of his food.

She served supper now with an injured air,

and John knew that she must be allowed to talk during the whole meal instead of only during the fish. She always talked during the fish. It was her ration. For she was lonely, poor thing, brooding all day in her basement. But when she was offended, or hurt, or merely annoyed, it was John's policy to allow her to exceed her ration.

So now she stood in the dark corner by the door, clutching an elbow feverishly in each hand, as if she feared that at any moment her forearms might fly away and be no more seen, and began:

'*Sack*, indeed! What next, I wonder? And I'm shore I hope you'll like the fillet of plaice, Mr Egerton, though reely I don't know *what* your tastes are. We all have our likes and dislikes as they say, and it takes time learning gentlemen's little ways. But as for seeing a sack in *this* house – well, I'm shore I don't know when you had it, Mr Egerton. A pore young thing that maid they have, so mean and scraggy-looking – a proper misery, *I* call her. And Mrs Byrne in that condition, too; one would think they wanted a good *strong* gairl to help about the house. The doctor was sent for this afternoon, Mr Egerton, and I don't wonder it came so soon, what with the worry about that other hussy going off like that – would you like the Worcester, Mr Egerton? You must *tell* me, you know, if there *is* anything.

105

I know the last gentleman would have mushroom catchup, or ketchop as they call it – nothing would satisfy him but mushroom catchup, and for those as like their insides messed up with toadstools and dandelions I'm shore it's very tasty, but, as I was saying, that Emily was a bad one and there's no mistake, gadding off like that with a young man and not her night out, and then the sauce of her people coming round and bothering Mrs Byrne about her – the idea. Cook tells me Mr Byrne told them straight out about her goings on with young men all the time she's been here, in and out, in and out night after night – and–'

John woke up with a start.

'What's that you say, Mrs Bantam? Mr Byrne – Mr Byrne did *what?*'

'I was just saying, sir, how Mr Byrne told Emily's people what he thought of her when they come worrying round the other day, so Cook was telling me. A proper hussy she must have been and no mistake – not Cook I mean, but that young Emily, gadding out night after night, young men and followers and the good Lord knows what all. Are you ready for your cutlet now, sir, and all that plaice left in the dish. Well. I never did, if you aren't a poor eater, Mr Egerton – and there's no doubt she was out with one of them one night and went further than she meant, no doubt, but if you make your bed you must lie on it, though I've no doubt she's sorry now...'

Mrs Bantam passed out into the kitchen, her voice trailing distantly away like the voices of the Pilgrims in *Tannhauser.*

John sat silent, pondering darkly her disclosures. It was a fortnight now since the fatal evening of Emily Gaunt's destruction and disposal. During the fortnight he had not once seen Stephen Byrne in private. They had met at the Underground Station; they had pressed against each other in the rattling train, shouting odd scraps of conversation with other members of The Chase; and John had marvelled at the easy cheerfulness of his friend. But since that night he had never 'dropped in' or 'looked in' at The House by the River in the evenings. He had never been asked to come, and he was glad. He was afraid of seeing Stephen alone, and he supposed that Stephen was afraid.

He had wondered sometimes what was going on in that house, had felt sometimes that he ought to go round and be helpful. But he could not. Like all The Chase, he had heard through his domestic staff of the sudden and inexcusable disappearance of Emily Gaunt. The soundless uncanny systems of communication, which the more skilled Indian tribes are reputed to employ, could not have disseminated with greater thoroughness or rapidity than Mrs Byrne's cook the precise details of the Emily mystery; how they had carried on angrily without her for three or four days, railing at her defection and lack of faith; how Mr Byrne had at last suggested that she might have met with an accident; how the police had been informed; how they had prowled about the garden and looked aimlessly under beds; how they had shaken their pompous heads again and gone away, and all the rest of it. There had been no explanation and few theories, so far, to account for the vanishing of Emily. Now Mrs Bantam had given him one, invented, apparently, and propagated by Stephen. And it shook him like a blow. That that poor girl – as good as gold, so far as he knew – should be slandered and vilified in death by the one man who should have taken care at least to keep her name clean. A fierce note of scorn and disgust broke involuntarily from him.

'Coming, sir,' cried Mrs Bantam, hurrying in with the almost imperceptible bustle of a swan pressed for time. 'And it's sorry I am it's only a couple of cutlets I'm giving you, brown and nice as they are, but could I get steak at the butcher's today? Not if I was the King of Spain, sir, no, and the loin-chop that scraggy it was a regular piece of profiteering to have it in the shop, that it was, let alone sell it. Well, sir, as my poor hubby used to say, that young woman's no better than she should be, and she's come to a bad end...'

'Never mind her now, Mrs Bantam. We

don't *know* anything–'

'*Know* anything! I should think not, sir, for they're all as deceiving and artful as each other, of course, and when a nice kind gentleman like Mr Byrne – but if one can't know one can guess – a nod's as good as a wink, they say, and I'm shore–'

The address continued interminably. John made himself as the deaf adder and scraped his cutlet clean in a mute fever of irritation. He felt as a man feels in a busy office, working against time at some urgent task in the face of constant interruptions. He could not fix his mind on the Emily matter, on Stephen, on the Underground Railway, or his food. There was a kind of thickness about his temples which he had noticed already at Turnham Green station, and he felt that he was not digesting. Mrs Bantam hammered ruthlessly on his tired head; and the ticket collector and the Board of Trade, and Emily and Stephen Byrne and the young porter at Victoria rushed indignantly about inside it. Sometimes he waved a fork distractedly at Mrs Bantam and asked her to fetch a new kind of sauce, to secure a moment's respite. Soon all the sauce bottles he possessed were ranged before him, a pitiful monument of failure. And when Mrs Bantam swept out to organize the sweet, he shouted that he had finished, and stole out into the garden, defeated.

It was a damp and misty evening, with a hint of rain. The tide was as it had been for a fortnight before on the Emily evening, rolling exuberantly in. Far out in the centre a dead yellow cat drifted westward at an astonishing speed, high out of the water. He knew the cat well. For weeks it had passed up and down the river. As far up as Richmond he had seen it, and as far down as London Bridge. Some days, perhaps, it caught under a moored barge, or was fixed for a little in the piers of a bridge, or ran ashore in the reeds above Putney, or lay at low tide under Hammerton Terrace. But most days it floated protesting through the Metropolis and back again. John wondered idly for how long it would drift like that, and in what last adventure it would finally disappear – cut in twain by a bustling tug, or stoned to the bottom by boys, or dragged down to the muddy depths by saturation. He thought of it straining now towards the sea, now to the open country, yet ever plucked back by the turning, relentless tide, just as it saw green fields or smelt the smell of the sea, to travel yet once more through the dark and cruel city. Once it was a kitten, fondled by children and very round and lovable and fat. And then the world had become indifferent, and then menacing, and then definitely hostile. Finally, no doubt, it had died a death of violence. John thought then of Emily, and sighed heavily. But he was feeling better now. Silence and the river had soothed him; and – given quiet and solitude – he had the Civil Servant's capacity for switching his mind from urgent worries to sedative thoughts. The cat, somehow, had been a sedative, in spite of its violent end. He went indoors out of the dark garden, studiously not looking at Stephen's windows.

While he was on the stairs the telephone-bell rang in his study. He took off the receiver and listened moodily to a profound silence, varied only by the sound of some one furtively picking a lock with the aid of a dynamo. Angrily he banged on the receiver and arranged himself in an arm-chair with a heavy book.

When he had done this the bell rang again. A petulant voice – no doubt justifiably petulant – said suddenly, 'Are you the Midland Railway?'

John said, 'No,' and rang off; then he thought of all the bitter and ironic things he ought to have said and regretted his haste.

He sat down and lit his pipe. The accursed bell rang again, insistently, with infinitesimal pauses between the rings. He got up violently, with a loud curse. The blood surged again in his head; the ticket collector and the maddening train and Mrs Bantam crowded back and concentrated themselves into the hateful exasperating shape of the telephone. He took off the receiver and shouted, *'Hullo! hullo!* What is it? What is it? Stop that ringing!' There was no answer; the bell continued to ring. He had banged his pipe against the instrument, and the first ash was scattered over the papers on the table. He took it out of his mouth, and furiously waggled the receiver bracket up and down. He had heard that this caused annoyance, if not actual pain, to the telephone operator, and he hoped fervently that this was true. He wanted to hurt somebody. He would have liked to pick up the instrument and hurl it in the composite face of the evening's per-secutors. His pipe rolled off on to the floor.

He shouted again, 'Oh, *what* is it? *Hullo! hullo! hullo!'*

The ringing abruptly ceased, and a low, anxious voice was heard: 'Hullo! hullo! hullo! Is that you, John? Hullo!' –Stephen's voice.

'Yes; what is it?'

'Can you come round a minute. I *must* see you. It's *urgent.'*

'What about?' said John, with a vague premonition.

'About – about – you know what! – about the other night – you *must* come! I can't leave the house.'

'No, I'm damned if I do – I've had enough of that.' At that moment John felt that he hated his old friend. The accumulated annoyances of the day merged in and reinforced the new indignation he had felt against Stephen since the sack incident and the revelations of Mrs Bantam. He had had enough. He refused to be further entangled in that business.

Then Stephen spoke again, appealingly, despairfully. 'John – you *must!* It's – it's *come up.*'

CHAPTER VI

John Egerton prepared himself to go round. He cursed himself for a weak fool; he reviled his fate, and Emily and Stephen Byrne. But he prepared himself. He was beaten.

But as he opened the front door the bell rang, and he saw Stephen himself on the doorstep – a pale and haggard Stephen, blinking weakly at the sudden blaze of light in the hall.

'I came round after all,' he said. 'It's urgent!' But he stepped in doubtfully.

The two curses of John Egerton's composition were his shyness and his soft-heartedness. When he saw Stephen he tried to look implacable; he tried to feel as angry as he had felt a moment before. But that weary and anxious face, that moment's hesitation on the step, and the whole shamefaced aspect of his friend melted him in a moment.

Something terrible must be going on to make the vital, confident Stephen Byrne look like that. Once more, he must be helped.

In the study, sipping like a wounded man at a comforting tumbler of whisky and water, Stephen told his story, beginning in the fashion of one dazed, with long pauses.

That evening just before dinner, as Mrs Bantam had correctly reported, the doctor had been sent for. And Stephen, waiting in the garden for his descent, gazing moodily through a thin drizzle at the grey rising river, had seen unmistakably fifty yards from the bank a semi-submerged object drifting rapidly past, wrapped up in sacking. A large bulge of sacking had shown above the surface. It was Emily Gaunt.

He was sure it was Emily Gaunt because of the colour of the sacking – a peculiar yellowish tint, unusual in sacks. And because he had always known it would happen. He had always known the rope would work on the flimsy stuff as the tide pulled, and eventually part it altogether. And now it had happened.

When he saw it he did not know what to do. 'I felt like rushing out into the boat at once,' Stephen said, 'and catching the thing – but the doctor ... Margery ... I had to wait...' he finished vaguely.

'Of course,' said John.

'When he came down he said all was well

– or fairly so – and he'd come again this evening. I'm expecting him now.' Then, with sudden energy, 'I wish to God he'd come... Is that *him?*' Stephen stopped and listened. John listened. There was no sound.

'But we mustn't waste time – half-past eight now – tide turning in a moment.' He leaned forward now, and began to speak with a jerky, almost incoherent haste, telescoping his words.

'When he'd gone I dashed down to the boat ... could still see the – the thing in the distance – going round the bend ... thought I'd catch it easily, but the engine wouldn't start – of COURSE! Took me half an hour ... starved for petrol, I think...' He stopped for a moment, as if still speculating on the precise malady of the engine.

'When I *did* get away ... went like a bird ... nearly up to Kew ... but not a sign of the – the sack ... looked everywhere ... couldn't wait any longer ... I *had* to get back ... only just back now ... against the tide. John, will *you* go out now? ... for God's sake, go ... take the boat and just patrol about ... slack water now ... tide turns in about ten minutes ... the damned thing *must* come down ... unless it's stuck somewhere ... you must go, John. We must get hold of it tonight ... tonight ... or they'll find it in the morning. And, John,' he added, as a hideous afterthought, his voice rising to a kind of hysterical shriek, 'there's a label on the sack – with my name and address – I remembered yesterday.'

'But ... but ...' began John.

'Quick! ... I've got to get back.' Stephen stood up. 'God knows what they think of me at home as it is... Say you'll go, John – *here's* the key of the boat ... she'll start at once now... It's a thousand to one chance, but it's worth it... And if you're not quick it'll go past again.'

Something of his old masterfulness was coming back with his excitement. But when John still hesitated, his slow mouth framing the beginnings of objection, the hunted look came upon Stephen again.

'John, for God's sake!' he said, with a low, pleading note. 'I'm about done, old man ... what with Margery and – and ... but there's still a chance ... John!'

The wretched John was melted again. He left his objections to the preposterous proposal unspoken. He put his hand affectionately on the other's shoulder.

'It's all right, Stephen ... I'll manage it somehow ... don't you worry, old boy ... I'll manage it.'

'Thank God! I'll go now, John ... I'll come down when I hear you come back ... I *must* go...'

Together they hurried down the stairs, and John found himself suddenly alone at the end of his garden in an old mackintosh, bemused and incredulous.

The rain had come, a hot, persistent, sibilant rain, and already it had brought the dark. The river was a shadowy mosaic of small splashes. The lights of Barnes showed mistily across the river, like lamps in a photograph. The tide was gathering momentum for the ebb; a mass of leaves and dead branches floated sluggishly past under the wall.

John was in the boat, fiddling stupidly at the engine, glistening and splashing in the rain, before he had thought at all what exactly he was going to do to discharge his fantastic undertaking. The engine started miraculously. John cast off and the boat headed doggedly up against the tide, John peering anxiously from side to side at the rain speckled water.

The engine roared and clattered; the boat vibrated, quivering all over; the oars and boathook rattled ceaselessly against the side of the boat – a hollow, monotonous rattle; the exhaust snorted rhythmically astern. The rain splashed and pattered on the engine and on the thwarts, and rolled with a luxurious swishing sound in the bottom. The flywheel of the engine revolved like a Catherine-wheel composed of water – water flying in brief tangents from the rim. John had come out without a hat, and his hair was matted and black; the river splashed on his neck and trickled slowly under his collar.

It was a heavy task, this, for one man with two hands to attempt, to shield the engine and himself with the same mackintosh, extending it like a wing with one arm over the flywheel; and to oil occasionally with an oil-can the mechanism of the pump, to regulate the oil-feed and the water-supply, and do all those little attentions without which the engine usually stopped; and at the same time to steer the boat, and look in the river for the floating body of a dead woman in a sack. It was madness. In that watery dusk his chances of seeing an obscure sack seemed ludicrously small. And what was he to do with it when he had found it? How should he dispose of it more effectually than it had been disposed of before? John did not know.

But the boat rattled and gurgled along, past the Island, and past the ferry, till they were level with the brewery, by the bend. The bend here made at one side a large stretch of slack water where the tide moved hardly at all. By the other bank the tide raced narrowly down. Here, John thought, was the place for his purpose. So for a long hour he steered the boat back and forth from bank to bank, peering intensely through the rain. Sometimes he saw a log or a basket or a broken bottle scurrying dimly past and chased it with a wild hope downstream. Once he made sure he had found what he had sought – a light object floating high out of the water; this he followed half-way down the Island. And when he found it it was a dead cat – a light-coloured cat. 'The yellow cat,' he thought. Once, as he headed obliquely across the river, boathook in hand, a black, invisible police-boat shot surprisingly across his bows. A curse came out of the gloom, and a lamp was flashed at him. The police-boat put about and worked back alongside; a heavy man in a cape asked him what the hell he was doing, charging about without a light. John might have asked the same question, but he was too frightened. He apologized and said he had let go of the rudder line to do something to the engine. The policeman went on again, growling.

Then the tugs began to come down, very comforting and friendly, their lights gliding mistily through the wet. John had to be careful then, and creep upstream along the bank while their long lines of barges swung ponderously round the corner. And how could he be sure that Emily was not slipping past him in midstream, as he did so? It was hopeless, this.

The wind got up – a chilly wind from the East. He was cold and clammy and terribly alone. The rain had crept under his shirt and up his sleeves; his trousers hung about his ankles, heavy with rain. He wanted to go home; he wanted to get out of the horrible

119

wet boat; he was tired. But he had promised. Stephen was his best friend, and Stephen had appealed to him. He had done a bad thing, but he was still Stephen.

And he, John, was mixed up in it now. If Emily was found at Putney in the morning, his own story would have to be told. Not a good story, either, whatever his motives had been. What *had* his motives been? Margery Byrne, chiefly of course. Well, she was still a motive – very much so.

But how futile the whole thing was, how wet and miserable and vile! It must have been something like this in the trenches, only worse. What was that going past? A bottle, a Bass bottle with a screw stopper, bobbing about like an old man walking. Ha-ha! What would he do when he found Emily? What the devil would he do? Sink her again? But he had no anchor now – nothing. Put her ashore on the Island? But somebody would find her. Take her out of the sack – the incriminating sack? If she was found by herself, a mere body, in a night-dress... In a nightdress? The night-dress wouldn't do. She mustn't be found in a night-dress? He would have to get rid of that too – that and the sack. Then anyone might find her, and it would be a mystery. And Stephen's stories... Stephen's stories about her levity and light conduct – they would come in useful. People like Mrs Bantam would quite understand, now they knew what sort of person Emily had been. John realized with a sudden shame that he was feeling glad that Stephen had said those things.

But how would he be able to do it? How could he take her out of the sack, out of the night-dress, and throw her back? How could he do it? and where? Once, long ago, he had come upon a big sack drifting in the evening. It was full of kindlewood, little penny packets of kindlewood, tied up with string. He remembered the weight of it, impossible to lift into the boat. He had towed it home, very slowly. He would have to tow Emily – land somewhere. She would be clammy and slippery – and disgusting. He couldn't do it. But he *must*. The engine stopped.

The engine stopped, mysteriously, abruptly. The boat slid sideways down the river. John pulled her head round with a paddle and fiddled gingerly with the hot engine. The rain fell upon it and sizzled. He turned vaguely a number of taps, fingered the electric wires; all was apparently well. He heaved at the starting-handle, patiently at first, then rapidly, then with a violent fury. Nothing happened. The boat slid along, turning sideways stupidly in the wind. They were almost level with The House by the River.

It was no good. John took the paddle and worked her laboriously across the tide. He had done his best, he felt. The rain had stopped.

When he came to the wooden steps the lights were on in Stephen's dining-room, in Stephen's drawing-room. And against the light he saw a head, motionless above the wall. The tide was a long way down now, faintly washing the bottom of the wall.

A hoarse whisper came over the water:

'John – John – any luck?'

'None, Stephen, I'm sorry.' John's voice was curiously soft and passionate.

There was silence. Then there came a kind of hysterical cackle, and Stephen's voice, 'John, it's – it's a boy!'

John stood up in the boat and began, 'Congratulations, old...'

There was another cackle, and the head was gone.

CHAPTER VII

Stephen Michael Hilary Byrne had given his mother the maximum of trouble that Friday evening; and on Sunday morning she was still too feeble and ill to appreciate his beauty. Old Dr Browning was less cheerful than Stephen had ever seen him. He shook his head almost grimly as he squeezed his square frame into his diminutive car.

Stephen went back disconsolately into the warm garden. He had seen Margery for a moment and she had whispered weakly, 'You go out in your boat, my dear,' and then something about 'a lovely morning ... I'm all right.' Also he had seen his son and tried hard to imagine that he was two years old, a legitimate object for enthusiasm. He had helped Joan to feed her rabbits and swept the garden and tidied things in the summer-house. But he had done all these things with an anxious eye on the full and falling river. And already he had had several shocks.

Now he felt that he could not leave the river, not at least while the tide was up and there was all this muddle of flotsam quivering past. Usually, on Sunday mornings he sat in his sunny window writing, with the birds bickering in the creeper outside and the lazy sounds of Sunday morning floating up from the river. Sunday morning along The Chase was an irreligious but peaceful occasion. The people of The Chase strolled luxuriously in the hot sun from door to door, watching their neighbours' children depart with fussy pomp upon their walks. Babies slept interminably in huge prams under the trees. The old houses looked very gracious and friendly with the wisteria and ivy and countless kinds of green things scrambling about the rickety balconies and wandering through the open windows. Strangers walked in quiet couples along the path and admired the red roofs and the quaint brass knockers on the doors and the nice old names of the houses and the nice old ladies purring sleepily inside. Out on the river the owners of the anchored boats prepared them happily for action, setting sails and oiling engines and hauling laboriously at anchors. Two white cutters moved delicately about in the almost imperceptible breeze. Strenuous eights and fours and pairs went rhythmically up and down. The hoarse adjurations of their trainers came over the water with startling clearness. Single scullers, contemptuously independent, shot by like large water-beetles in slim skiffs. On the far towpath the idle people streamed blissfully along, marvelling at the gratuitous exertions of the oarsmen. Down the river there was a multitude of small boys bathing from a raft, with much splashing and shrill cries. Their bodies shone like polished metal in the distance. There were no tugs on Sundays, but at intervals a river-steamer plodded up towards Kew, a congested muddle of straw hats and blouses. Sometimes a piano tinkled in the stern, sounding almost beautiful across the water.

On all these vulgar and suburban and irreligious people the June sun looked down with a great kindness and warmth; and they were happy. And Stephen, as a rule, was happy at Hammersmith on Sunday mornings. He thought with repugnance of Sunday mornings in Kensington, of stiff clothes in the High Street and the shuttered faces of large drapery stores; he thought with pity even of the promenaders in Hyde Park, unable to see the trees for people, unable to look at the sky because of their collars. He loved the air and openness and pleasant vulgar variety of Sunday morning at Hammersmith. Here at least it was a day of naturalness and rest. On any other Sunday, if the tide served, he would have slipped out after breakfast in his boat to gather firewood for the winter. Just now there was a wealth of driftwood in the river, swept off wharves by the high spring tides or flung away by bargees – wedges and small logs and boxwood and beams and huge stakes, and delicious planks covered with tar. Anyone who had a boat went wood-hunting on the river.

He had a mind to go now. But it would look so odd, with his wife dangerously ill indoors, though she herself had told him to do it. But then that was like her. He must not go unless he had to – unless he saw something... All Saturday while the tide was up he had furtively watched from window or garden, and seen nothing. Perhaps he had made a mistake on Friday.

No. He had made no mistake. Emily Gaunt was drifting somewhere in this damnably public river. Unless she was already found, already lying in a mortuary. And if she was–

Stephen looked enviously at the happy crowds on the towpath, on the steamers, in the boats. A heavy sculling-boat passed close to the wall. It seemed almost to overflow with young men and women. All of them gazed curiously at him, muttering comments on his appearance. Their easy laughter annoyed him. He went indoors.

He sat down automatically at his table in the window, and took out of a pigeon-hole a crumpled bundle of scribbled paper. It was the beginning of a long poem. He had begun it – when? Two – three weeks ago. Before Emily. He read through what he had written, and thought it was bad – weak, flabby, uneven stuff – as it stood. But it was a good idea, and he could do it justice, he was sure, if he persevered. But not now. Just now he was incapable. Since Emily's night he had not written a line of poetry; he had only tried once. Not because of his conscience – it was the anxiety, the worry. He could not concentrate.

A bell rang below, and he wondered if it was John Egerton. There was the sound of conversation in the hall, Cook's voice and the voice of a man, powerful and low. Then Cook lumbered up the stairs.

'If you please, sir, there's a man brought the sack back what Mr Egerton took, as used to 'ang in the scullery, and 'e'd like to see you.'

Stephen braced himself and went down. The man in the hall was an obvious detective – square built and solid, with hard grey eyes and a dark walrus moustache, a bowler hat in his hand. In the other he held the end of a yellow sack, muddy in patches and discoloured.

'Sorry to trouble you, sir, but can you tell me anything about this sack? I'm a police officer,' he added unnecessarily.

Stephen felt extraordinarily cool.

He said, 'Can't say, Inspector. Sacks are very much alike. We had one in the scullery once, but–' He had the sack in his hands now, looking for the label.

'And what happened to *your* sack, sir?' said the man smoothly.

'We lent it to Mr Egerton, and – *Hullo!* where did you find *this*, Inspector? It *is* ours!' And he held it out for the other to see the blurred lines of the label stitched inside the mouth of the sack. The name of Stephen Byrne, The House by the River, W6, was still legible.

'Very curious, sir,' said the man, looking hard at Stephen. 'Do you remember when you lent it to Mr Egerton?'

Stephen made a rapid calculation. The exact period was seventeen days.

He said, 'When was it, Cook? About three

weeks ago, wasn't it?'

'Couldn't say, sir, I'm sure. All I knows is it went one day, and the other day we asked for it back from Mr Egerton when the man came about the bottles, and he said – Mr Egerton said, that is – as he was sorry he'd lost it picking up wood, or so Mabel said, and it was Mabel as went round for it.'

Stephen was feeling cooler and cooler. It was all amazingly easy.

He said, 'That's right, Cook; I remember now. I gave it to Mr Egerton myself one evening; he was going out to get wood.' Then, with a tone of cheerful finality as one who puts an end to a tedious conversation with an inferior, 'Well, I'm sure we're much obliged to you, Inspector, for bringing it back. Where–'

'If you don't mind, sir, I'd like to keep it a little longer. Those are my orders, sir – there's a little matter we're clearing up just now–'

'Just so. Certainly, Inspector. As long as you like.'

'Thank you, sir. And as I take it, sir, none of your household has seen anything of this article since you lent it to Mr Egerton?'

'As far as I know, no one – I certainly haven't seen it myself. In fact, I was looking for it only the other day.'

The Inspector thought obviously for a moment, and obviously decided to say no more. 'Well, that's all, sir, and thank you.'

Stephen bowed him affably out of the door. 'Of course, if it's anything *important*, I should look in and see Mr Egerton – he's only next door.'

'No, sir, it's of no consequence. I'll be off now.'

The man departed, with many smiles, and 'sirs', and 'Thank yous', and Stephen watched him round the corner.

Then he went into the garden, full of a curious relief, almost of exultation. He could delight at last in the sun and the boats and the happy, irresponsible people. He, too, could look at the beloved river without any urgent anxiety of whatever it might carry into his view. The worst was over; the doubts were done with him. Emily was found, and there was an end to it. And he had diddled the policeman. How cleverly, how gloriously he had diddled the policeman. Perfect frankness and easiness and calm – a gracious manner and a good lie – they had worked perfectly. He had never hoped for anything so easy. Almost without intention, certainly without plan, as if inspired he had uttered those tremendous lies about John. And, of course, he could hardly have said anything else. Cook had given John away already; one must be consistent. Poor old John! He must see John – talk to him – warn him – no, diddle him. He could manage John all right.

He went down the steps into his tiny dinghy – a minute, fragile, flat-bottomed affair, just large enough and strong enough for a single man. It flitted lightly on the surface like one of those cumbrous-looking water flies which move suddenly on the quiet surface of ponds with a startling velocity. He called it *The Water Beetle*.

With a few strokes Stephen shot out into the lovely sun, and drifted a little, faintly stirring the oars as they rested flatly on the golden water with a movement which was almost a caress. It was very delightful out there, very soothing and warm. It was inspiring, too. Stephen suddenly thought of the long poem. He must have a go at that – now that things were better, now that his mind was easier.

Then he saw John walk down to the end of his garden, smoking comfortably the unique and wonderful Sunday morning pipe. He rowed back immediately to the wall, framing smooth explanatory phrases in his head. John, he saw, was gazing with a strained look through his glasses at a muddle of wreckage drifting down from the Island.

'You needn't worry, John,' he said; 'it's all over – it's – it's *found*... Come down the steps.'

John came down and squatted at the foot of the steps, saying nothing. Stephen tied up the boat, but did not get out of it.

'A man's been here this morning – a policeman – with the sack ... he wanted to know if we knew anything about it ... Cook saw him first, and let out that it was ours – said we'd lent it to you – silly fool ... about three weeks back ... when I saw him it was too late to say anything else...' He stopped and looked up. Surely John was going to say something.

John looked steadily at him and said nothing.

'She said Mabel went round and asked you for it, and you said – what *did* you say, John?'

John looked out across the river and thought. Then he said in a far-away voice:

'I said I'd taken it out to pick up wood – and lost it. Overboard ... I had to say something.'

'Hell!' Stephen hoped that this exclamation had an authentic note of perplexity and distress. He was conscious of neither, only of a singular clearness and contentment.

'Well, what are we going to do now?' There was no answer.

'Margery's very bad this morning,' he went on, with seeming irrelevance 'We're very worried. The doctor...'

John interrupted suddenly. 'What *can* we do? What will the police do next? Will they come and see me?' He had a sudden appalling vision of himself in a stammering, degrading interview with a detective.

'No, John, they won't bother you... I'm the man they'll bother... There'll be an inquest, of course... And I'm afraid you'll have to give evidence, John ... say what you said before, you know ... say you lost it ... about three weeks ago ... that's what I said ... somebody must have picked it up... I'm awfully sorry, John – but it will be all right...' Then, doubtfully, 'Of course, John ... if you'd rather ... I'll go at once and tell them the whole thing ... I hate the idea of you ... but there's Margery... The doctor said ... I don't know what would happen...'

John was roused at last. 'Of course not, Stephen ... you're not to think of it ... it'll be all right, as you say... Only ... only...' with a strange fierceness, 'I wish to God it had never happened.' And he looked at Stephen very straight and stern, almost comically stern.

'So do I,' said Stephen, with a heavy sigh. For the first time since the policeman left he had the old sense of guiltiness and gloom.

'There's one thing, Stephen...' John hesitated and stammered a little. 'I've heard some awful rumours about ... about that girl ... immoral and so on ... they're not true, are they? ... anyhow, don't let's encourage them, Stephen ... it's not necessary ... and I don't like it...' He stopped, and was aware that he was blushing. It was a lame presentation of what he had intended as a firm unanswerable ultimatum: 'If you want me to help you, you must drop all this.' But Stephen somehow always intimidated him.

Stephen thought, 'The damned old prig!' He said, 'What *do* you mean, John? You don't imagine I ... these servants, I suppose ... but I quite agree ... I must go and see Margery now. So long, John ... and thank you so much.'

John went up into his garden and into his house and sat for a long time in a leather chair thinking and wondering. Stephen walked briskly in and whispered to the nurse. Mrs Byrne was asleep.

He sat down at the sunny table in the study window, and drew out again the long poem. It was a good idea – a very good idea. He read through what he had written; uneven, yes, but there was good stuff in it. A little polishing up wanted, a little correction. All that bit in the middle... He scratched out 'white' and scribbled over it 'pale'. Yes, that was better. The next part, about the snow, was rather wordy – wanted condensing; there were six lines, and four at least were very good – but one of them must go – perhaps two. He sharpened a pencil, looking out at the river.

CHAPTER VIII

After the inquest The Chase had plenty to talk about. Mrs Ambrose and Mrs Church were kept very busy. For few of The Chase had been actually present in the flesh – not because they were not interested and curious and indeed aching to be present, but because it seemed hardly decent. Since the great Nuisance Case about the noise of the Quick Boat Company's motor-boats there had been no event of communal importance to The Chase; life had been a lamentable blank. And it was an ill-chance that the first genuine excitement, not counting the close of the Great War, should be a function which it seemed hardly decent to attend: an inquest on the dead body of a housemaid from The Chase discovered almost naked in a sack by a police-boat at Barnes. Nevertheless, a sprinkling of The Chase was there – Mrs Vincent for one, and Horace Dimple, the barrister, for another – though he of course attended the inquest purely as a matter of professional interest, in the same laudable spirit of inquiry in which law students crowd to the more sensational or objectionable trials at the High Court. There were also Mr

Mard, the architect, who was on the Borough Council, and Mr and Mrs Tatham, who had to visit the Food Committee that day. These, being in the neighbourhood of the Court, thought it would be foolish not to 'look in'. Few of them overtly acknowledged that the others were visibly there, or, if they were compelled to take notice, smiled thinly and looked faintly surprised.

But so startling and sensational was the course of the inquest that when they returned to their homes any doubts about the propriety of attending it were speedily smothered by the important fact that they had positively been there, had been eye-witnesses of the astonishing scene, whether from chance or compassion or curiosity, or wisdom, or the simple power of divination, which most of them felt they must un-doubtedly possess. They had known all along that there was 'something fishy' about that girl's disappearance, and now, you see, they were right. They looked eagerly in the morning papers and in the evening papers as only those look who have seen something actually take place, and insanely crave to see it reported in dirty print in the obscure corners of a newspaper. So do men who happen on a day to hear part of a Parlia-mentary debate anxiously study on the morrow the Parliamentary reports at which they never so much as glanced before, and are never likely to glance again... But this is human nature, and we must not be unkind to The Chase because they were unable to depart from that high standard.

The papers reported the affair with curious brevity and curiously failed to get at the heart of it. The headlines were all about 'Mr Stephen Byrne' – 'Poet's Housemaid' – 'Tragedy in an Author's House' – and so on. It was only at the end of the small paragraphs that you found out there were black suspicions about a Civil Servant, one John Egerton, first-class clerk in the Ministry of Drains. And for The Chase these suspicions were the really startling and enthralling outcome of the inquest, as Mrs Vincent and others described it. Mrs Vincent described it after dinner in the house of the Petways where she had dropped in casually for a chat. By a curious chance Mr Dimple had also dropped in, so that the fortunate Petways had two eyewitnesses at once. The Whittakers came in in the middle of the story.

And they all agreed that it was a surprising story – highly surprising as it affected Mr Egerton, and also highly unfavorable. Dear Mr Byrne had given his evidence in his usual charming manner, very clear and straightforward and delightful: very anxious to help the Coroner and the jury, in spite of the worry about poor Mrs Byrne. 'Very pale he was,' said Mrs Vincent. 'Overstrained,' said Mr Dimple.

And it all depended on this sack, you see. The girl was tied up in the sack. Mrs Vincent gave a little shiver. 'Of course, it was all *rather* horrible, you know, but–' 'But you enjoyed it thoroughly,' thought Whittaker.

'Mr Byrne said he remembered lending the sack to Mr Egerton – to collect firewood or something – you know, he's *always* poking about in that silly boat of his, picking up sticks.' (The operation as described by Mrs Vincent sounded incredibly puerile and base.) 'Then the Coroner asked him if he remembered *when*. Mr Byrne said it was about three weeks ago. Then they asked was it before or after the day that this young woman disappeared. You could have heard a pin drop.

'I was really sorry for Mr Byrne; I could see he didn't like it a bit. He didn't answer for a little, kind of hesitated, then he said it was *about* the same day – he couldn't be sure; and that was all they could get out of him – it was *about* the same day. And you should have *seen* Mr Egerton's face.'

Mrs Vincent paused to appreciate the effect of her narrative.

'Then there was the Byrnes' young woman, Mabel Jones or some such name. She was sent round to Mr Egerton's to ask for the sack – one day last week. And *she* said – what was it she said, Mr Dimple?'

137

'She said Mr Egerton was "short like" with her, and–'

'Ah, yes!' Mrs Vincent hastened to resume the reins. 'He was "short like" and a bit 'uffy with her; and he said he'd lost the sack, picking up wood – lost it in the river...

'And then Mr Egerton himself was put in the box and he told *exactly the same story!*' Mrs Vincent said these words with a huge ironical emphasis, as if it would have reflected credit on Mr Egerton had he invented an entirely new story for the purposes of the inquest.

'He told exactly the same story, and he told it very badly, in my opinion – *you* know, hesitating and mumbling, as if he was keeping something back – and looking at the floor all the time.'

'We must remember he's naturally a very shy man,' said Mr Dimple, 'and a public inquest, at the best–'

'Yes, but look what he *said*– The Coroner asked him the same question – when was it he had borrowed the sack – before or after the young woman disappeared. Mr Egerton said he really didn't know, because he didn't know when the young woman had disappeared... As if we didn't *all* know, the very next day...'

'Pardon me,' said Mr Dimple, 'but I didn't know myself, not till one day last week – and I live two doors from the Byrnes–'

'Yes, but you're a *man*,' said Mrs Vincent, with a large contempt.

'So is Mr Egerton.'

Mrs Vincent should have been a boxer. She recovered nobly.

'Anyhow, he didn't impress me, and he didn't impress the Coroner. The Coroner kept at him a long time, trying to get it out of him, *how* he'd lost the sack and so on. Some of the jury asked questions too. They couldn't understand about the wood-collecting and what he wanted firewood for in the summer, and– Oh yes, *I* remember. He said it must have slipped off the boat, you see, and been picked up by somebody. Then they asked him what he did with the wood when he picked it up – did he put it in the sack then and there or what? He said no, he just threw it in the bottom of the boat. *Then* the Coroner said, 'When did you put it in the sack?' Mr Egerton said, 'In the garden, of course, to take it indoors.' And then, you see, the Coroner said, 'Why on earth did he take the sack out in the boat at *all?*' You could have heard a–' Mrs Vincent thought better of it. 'Mr Egerton couldn't answer that – he just looked sheepish, and mumbled something about "he forgot!" – forgot, indeed!'

Mrs Vincent looked at Mr Dimple – a triumphant, merciless look.

Mr Dimple murmured reflectively, 'Yes – that *was* odd – very odd.'

139

'And as for that Mrs Bantam of his, the old frump! *She* actually swore that there'd never been a sack in the house! Well, it stands to reason, if Mr Egerton borrowed that sack to collect wood in, she *must* have seen it, unless he kept it locked up somewhere – and if he did lock it up somewhere – well, he must have had some funny reason for it...'

Mrs Vincent shrugged her shoulders expressively.

'So *that* didn't do him any good – especially as she cheeked the Coroner.'

'And what was the verdict?'

'Oh, the jury were *very* quick – I only waited ten minutes or so, you know, just on chance – and when they came back they said. "Wilful murder against somebody unknown" – or something like that. I must say, I was surprised, because the Coroner was *very* down on Mr Egerton–'

'And so were you, I gather,' said Mrs Whittaker, with forced calm; the Whittakers liked Egerton, and Mrs Vincent was slowly bringing them to the boil.

'Well, if you ask me, I really *don't* think he comes out of it very well. Of course, I know the jury didn't say anything about him, but–'

'And that being so, Mrs Vincent, if you will allow me!' – Mr Dimple at last cast off his judicial detachment; he spoke with his usual deprecating and kindly air, with a kind of halting fluency that made it seem as if his sentences would never end – 'if you will allow me – er, as a lawyer – to ah, venture a little advice – that being so, I think one ought to be careful – not to say anything – which might be – ah, repeated – by perhaps thoughtless people – of course I know we are all friends here –and possibly misinterpreted – as a suggestion – that Mr Egerton's part in this affair – though I know, of course, that there were – er – puzzling circumstances – about the evidence – I thought so myself – that Mr Egerton's part – was – er – more serious – than one is entitled strictly to deduce – from the verdict – which *as* you say – Mrs Vincent – did not refer to him directly in any way. You won't mind me saying so, will you? – but I almost think–'

Mr Dimple always talked like that. He was a noble little man, with a thin, peaked legal countenance and mild eyes that expressed unutterable kindness and impartiality to the whole world. His natural benevolence and a long training in the law had produced in him a complete incapacity for downright censure. His judgments were a tangle of parentheses; and people said that if he were ever raised to the Bench his delivery of the death sentence would generate in the condemned person a positive glow of righteousness and content. He never 'thought' or 'said'; he only 'almost thought' or 'ventured

141

to suggest' or 'hazarded the opinion, subject of course to–' And this, combined with his habit of parenthesis and periphrasis and polysyllaby (if there is a word like that), made his utterances of almost unendurable duration. He was one of those men during whose anecdotes it is almost impossible to keep awake. Polite people, who knew him well and honoured him for the goodness of his heart and the charity of his life, sometimes rebuked themselves because of this failure, and swore to do better when they met him again. At the beginning of a story (and he had many) they would say to themselves firmly, 'I will keep awake during the whole of this anecdote; I will attend to the very end; I will understand it and laugh sincerely about it.' Then Mr Dimple would ramble off into his genial forest of qualifications and brackets, and the minds of his hearers immediately left him; they thought of their homes, or their work, or the food they were eating, or of the clothes of some other person, or of some story they intended to tell when Mr Dimple had done; and they came suddenly out of their dreams, to find Mr Dimple yet labouring onward to his climax; and they said, with shame and mortification, 'I have failed again,' and laughed very heartily at the wrong moment.

Yet people loved Mr Dimple; and if it was impossible sometimes to deduce from what he actually said what it was he actually thought, one was often able to make a good guess on the assumption that he never wittingly said anything cruel or unkind or even mildly censorious to or about anybody.

Mr Whittaker knew this, and he interrupted with: 'Thank you, Dimple – I thoroughly agree with you – but I don't think you go nearly far enough.' He stood up, looking very severely at Mrs Vincent. 'I think it's *disgusting* to say such things about a man – especially about a man like Egerton. I think we ought to get home now, Dorothy. Good night, Mrs Petway.'

Mrs Petway spluttered feebly, but was unable to utter. The Whittakers departed, trailing clouds of anger.

Mrs Vincent assumed an air of injury.

'Well, my dear, I'm sure I'm sorry if I said anything to upset them, but really– Of course, I know I don't understand the *law*, Mr Dimple, and I don't want to be unfair to any man, but one must use one's common sense, and what I think is that Mr Egerton made away with the poor girl, and that's all about it.'

She looked defiantly at Mr Dimple. Mr Dimple opened his mouth and shut it again. Then he went away.

CHAPTER IX

It is to be regretted that very many of The Chase shared the views of Mrs Vincent. Mrs Vincent was a tireless propagandist of her own views about other people. The Whittakers, and the Dimples, and the Tathams, and all the more charitable and kindly people who were faintly shocked but unconvinced by the whole affair, preferred not to talk about it at all. So Mrs Vincent steadily gained ground and John Egerton became a dark and suspected figure, regarded with a shuddering horror by most of his neighbours. He found this out very soon at the Underground station in the mornings. Here on the platform there were always many of The Chase, watching with growing irritation the non-stop trains thundering past, and meanwhile chattering with one another of their hopes and fears and domestic crises. John soon found that men became engrossed in advertisements or conversations or newspapers as he approached, or sidled away down the platform, or busily lit their pipes. And twice, before he realized what was in their minds, his usual 'Good morning' was met with a stony, contemp-

144

tuous stare. After that he took to avoiding the men himself. He noticed then that the burly and genial ticket collector had begun to withhold his invariable greeting and comment on the weather. And after that John travelled by bus to Hammersmith and took the train there. Nobody knew him there. And he left off walking up the Square, but went by Red Man Lane, which was longer. In the Square he might meet anybody. In the Square everybody knew him. In the Square he felt that every one discussed him as he passed; the women chattering at their cottage doors lowered their voices, he was sure, and muttered about him. The milk-boys stared at him unusually, and laughed suddenly, contemptuously, when he had gone. Or so he thought. For he was never sure. He felt sometimes that he would like to stop and make sure. He would like to say to the two young women with the baskets whom he passed every day, 'I believe you were saying something about me... I know what it was... Well, it's all rot... It was another man did it, really... I can't explain ... but you've no right to look at me like that.' He longed to be able to justify himself, for he was a warm and sympathetic soul, and liked to be on terms of vague friendliness, and respect with people he met or passed in the streets or dealt with daily in shops; he liked saying

'Good morning' to milkmen and porters and policemen and paper-boys. And the fear that any day any of these people might ignore him or insult him was a terrible fear.

Contrary to the common belief, it is more difficult for an innocent man, if he be shy and sensitive, to look the whole world in the face than it is for the abandoned evil-doer with his guilt fresh up him. So John avoided people he knew as much as he could. He avoided even his friends. The kindly Whittakers made special efforts to bring him to their house. They urged him to come in on their Wednesday evenings that they might show the Vincents and the Vincent following what decent people thought of him. But he would not go. He could not face the possibility of a public insult in a drawing-room, some degrading, hot-cheeked, horrible 'scene'.

And after all, it was only for a little time. Mrs Byrne was still in a bad way, but she was 'out of the wood', Mrs Bantam said. And when she was quite well, Stephen of course would somehow manage to put things right, in spite of his extraordinary conduct at the inquest. He did not see Stephen for ten days after the inquest. He had felt sometimes that he would like to see him, would like to tell him how awkward he had made things by the way he had given his evidence. But it seemed hardly fair to worry him. He must be worried enough, as it was, poor man. And

John felt that he would never be able to approach the topic without seeming to be questioning Stephen's loyalty. And he did not want to do that. He was quite sure that Stephen had never meant to put things as he had. It was nervousness; and the muddle-headedness that come from too much thinking, too much planning, and the musty, intimidating atmosphere of the Coroner's Court, and the stupid badgering of the smug Coroner. Probably Stephen had hardly known what he was saying. He himself had felt like that. And Stephen had had far more reason for nervousness in that place. When Margery was better, he would go round and see Stephen, and Stephen would 'do the right thing'. That was his own phrase. Meanwhile, people must be avoided, and Mrs Bantam was a great comfort. Mrs Bantam had shown herself a loyal and devoted soul. She, at least, had perfect faith in him. There had never been a sack in *this* house, *that* she knew. And that was all about it. Since her spirited appearance in the Coroner's Court, her inter-prandial addresses were confined to two themes – the ineptitude of the law and the high character of her employer. She was wearisome, but she was very soothing to the injured pride of a shy man who conceived himself as the detested byword of West London.

There was one other spark of comfort. The

Tarrants were away in the country and had missed all this. But Mrs Vincent was a friend of Mrs Tarrant and would no doubt write to her. John wondered whether he ought to write to Muriel Tarrant. He did not think so. They were not really on writing terms.

And in the big room over the river, where the blinds were always down, but the sun thrust through in brilliant slices at the corners, Margery Byrne lay very still – sleeping and thinking, sleeping and thinking, of Stephen and Michael Hilary and Joan, but chiefly of Stephen. In the morning and in the evening he came up and sat with her for an hour, and he was very tender and solicitous. She saw that he was pale and weary looking, with anxious eyes, and she was touched and secretly surprised that her illness should have made him look like this. Indeed, it pleased her. But she told him that he must worry about her no more; she told him he must eat enough, and not sit up working too late. Then she would say that she wanted to sleep, lest he should become fidgety or bored with sitting in the darkened room. She would kiss him very fondly, and follow him with her eyes while he walked softly to the door. Then she would lie in a happy dream listening to the birds in the ivy, and the soft river-sounds, the distant cries of the bargemen, and the melancholy whistle of tugs, and the ripple of their wash about the moored boats; she would lie and listen and make huge plans for the future – infinite, impossible, contradictory plans. And the centre of all of them was Stephen.

And Stephen would go down into the warm study and sit down in the study window and write. Even since that Sunday morning when the detective came with the sack he had been writing. It was extraordinary that he was able to write. He knew that it was extraordinary. Sometimes he sat in the evening and tried to understand it. In that fearful time before the detective came, and most of all in those terrible days when Emily Gaunt was drifting irrecoverably up and down the river, no conceivable power could have wrung from him a single line. He could no more have written poetry than he could have written a scientific treatise. But now, amazingly, he could command the spirit, the idea, the concentration – everything; he could become absorbed, could lose himself in his work. The idea he was working on had been with him for a long time; he had made notes for the poem many weeks back, long before Emily had come to the house; he had written a few lines of it just before she left it. But one wanted more than ideas to do good work of that kind; one must have – what was it? – 'peace of mind', presumably. There must be no tempers, or terrors, or worries in the mind. And, one would have thought, no remorse, no pricking of conscience. But perhaps that did not matter. For otherwise how could he now have 'peace of mind'? Stephen felt that his conscience was working; he was sorry for what he had done – truly sorry. He was sorry for poor old John. But it did not trouble him when he sat down in the sunshine to write. He could forget it then. But that day when the baby came, when he had seen the sack go past and chased it in the boat, and the next day when Emily was still at large, drifting bulkily for the first police-boat to see – on those days he could not have forgotten. He had been afraid – afraid for Margery, and afraid for himself. And now, somehow, he was not afraid. Why was that? Distressing things, appalling things, might still happen, but he was not disturbed by them. The day after the inquest he had been a little disturbed; he had not been able to settle down to work that day; he had wandered vaguely up and down the house, had sat in the garden a little, had rowed in the boat a little – restless; and he had slept badly. But the next day he had worked successfully many hours. In a little diary he kept a record of work – so many hours, such and such a poem, so many hundreds of words. All these weeks he had automatically made the entries as usual, and from Sunday, 1st June, the figures moved steadily upward. After the 5th there was a distinct bound – seven hours on the 6th. June 1st was the day the policeman came – the day he had told the policeman about John – almost by accident, he felt. Yes; he had not meant anything then. And the 4th was the day of the inquest – the day he had made all those other suggestions about John – quite unintentionally – and cleverly, too. That was the secret of it, of course, that was the real foundation of his peace of mind – the way he had managed to entangle John in the affair. He had John hopelessly entangled now.

It was strange how it had worked out. In the beginning he had honestly intended 'to do the right thing'. Or he believed he had. From the time, at any rate, that John had become seriously involved, he had really meant to 'own up' as soon as Margery was well enough. Probably it would have meant suicide, he remembered – a long time ago it seemed – thinking of that; but he was going to do *something*. And then the inspiration and the chance had come hand in hand that Sunday morning to show him a better way. It *was* a better way. He knew quite certainly now that he would never own up – not even if Margery was to die. He would never say a word to clear John's character. He had a fairly clear idea now of what would happen. There would (he hoped) be no further proceedings; the evidence was too thin. All that John would suffer would be this local gossip and petty suspicion; and he would have to live that down. John would not mind – a good fellow, John. But if he did mind, if he ever showed signs of expecting to be cleared, if he ever suggested a confession or any rubbish of that sort, the answer would be simple; 'Really, my dear John, the evidence is so strong against you that I don't really think I should be *believed* now if I said *I* did it. And you must remember, John, you've anyhow sworn all sorts of things on your oath that you'd have to explain away – the Civil Service wouldn't like that – perjury, you know. Of course, if you *want* me, John – but I really think it would be better from *your* point of view – I only want to do the best for *you*, John–'

He could hear himself solemnly developing the argument; and he could see John bowing to his judgment, acquiescing.

If he didn't acquiesce; if he made trouble, or if the police made trouble – but Stephen preferred not to think of that. Yet if it did happen he would be ready. If it was oath against oath, with the scales weighted already against John, he knew who would be believed.

And, after all, John Egerton, good fellow as he was, would leave but a tiny gap in the world. What were his claims on life? What had he to give to mankind? A single man, parents dead, an obscure Civil Servant, at five hundred a year – a mere machine, incapable of creation, easily replaced, perhaps not even missed. What was he worth to the world beside the great Stephen Byrne? Supposing they both died now, how would their obituary notices compare? John's – but John would not have one; his death would be announced on the front page of the newspapers. But about himself there would be half columns. He knew what they would say: 'Tragic death of a young poet still in his prime ... Keats ... unquestionable stamp of genius ... a loss that cannot be measured ... best work still unwritten ... engaged, we understand ... new poem ... would have set the seal...' and so on.

And it would all be true. Wasn't it *right*, then, that if the choice had ever to be made, he, Stephen Byrne, should be chosen, should be allowed to live and enrich the world? It was curious that never before had he so clearly appreciated his own value to humanity. Somehow, he had never thought of himself in that way. This business had brought it home to him.

Anyhow, he must get on with this poem. It was going to be a big thing. The more he wrote, the more it excited him; and the more contented he became with the work he was doing, the more satisfied he was with his material circumstances, the more sure that all would be well for him with the Emily affair.

This is the way of many writers. Their muses and their moods react upon each other in a kind of unending circle. When they are unhappy they cannot write; but when they are busy with writing, and they know that it is good, they grow happier and happier. Then when they have finished and the first intoxication of achievement has worked itself out, depression comes again. And then, while they are yet too exhausted for a new effort, all their work seems futile and worthless, and all life a meaningless blank. And until the next creative impulse restores their confidence and vigour they are, comparatively, miserable.

Stephen Byrne was peculiarly sensitive to these reactions. He had that creative itch which besets especially the young writer with his wings still strange and wonderful upon him. At the end of a day in which he had written nothing new, he went to bed with a sense of frustration, of failure and emptiness. There was something missing. For weeks on end he wrote something every day, some new created thing, if it was only a single verse apart from the routine work of criticism and review-writing and odd journalism with which he helped to keep his family alive. But ideas do not come continually to any man; and when they come, the weary mind is not always ready to shape them.

There were long periods of barrenness or stagnancy when Stephen could write nothing. Sometimes the ideas came copiously enough, but hovered like maddening ghosts just out of his grasp, clearly seen, but unattainable. Sometimes they came not at all. In either case, like a good artist, Stephen made no attempt to force the unwilling growth, but let himself lie fallow for a while. But all those fallow times he was restless and half-content. He had the sense, somehow, of failure. He became moody and irritable, and silent at meals. But when the creative fit was upon him, when he had made some little poem, or was still hot and busy at a long one, the world was benevolent and good, life was a happy adventure, and Stephen talked like a small boy at dinner-time.

So this poem he was working at was an important thing. The 'idea' was comparatively old. It had come to him in a fallow time, and had been stored somewhere away. When the policeman's visit restored his tranquillity, the fallow time was over. The idea was ready to hand, and he had only to take it out and sow it and water it. And as it grew and blossomed under his hand, it commanded him. It made him superior to circumstance; it decorated his fortunes and made them hopeful and benign. Nothing could be harmful or disturbing while he was doing such good work every day. It made him sure that he was right – sure that his decisions were wise. It made him see that no good purpose would be served by telling the world the truth about Emily Gaunt and about John Egerton. So he went on writing.

But there was another curious thing about this poem. It was a kind of epic, an immensely daring, ambitious affair. The war came into it, but it was not about the war. Rather it was a great song of the chivalry and courage of the men and women of our time wherever these have appeared. There were battles in it, and the sea was in it, and something of the obscure gallantry of hidden or humble men; and something also of the imperishable heroisms that did not belong to the war – Scott's last voyage and Shackleton's voyage, and the amazing braveries of the air.

And day by day as he sat there in the sun, glorifying, page by page, the high qualities of these men, their courage and their truth and straightness, he was conscious distantly of the strange contradiction between what he was doing and what he was. He stopped sometimes and thought, 'This is sincere work that I am doing; I mean it; it excites me; the critics, whatever they say, will say that it is sincere and noble writing. Parents in the days to come may make their children read it as an exhortation to manliness and truth. They may even say that I was a noble character myself... And all the time I am doing a mean and dirty thing – a cowardly thing. And I don't care. My life is a lie, and this poem is a lie, but I don't care; it is good work.'

All that June the weather was very lovely. In the busy streets the air grew heavy and stifling, full of dust and the vile fumes of motor buses. They were like prisons. But by the river there was always a sense of freshness and freedom; and when the great tide swept up in the evenings a gentle breeze came in light breaths from the west and fingered and fondled the urgent water, making it into a patchwork of rippled places and smooth places, where there swam for a little in a fugitive glow of amber and rose the small clouds over the Richmond Hills. Then it was cool and strengthening to sit in a small boat and drink the breeze, and Stephen always, when the tide was up, would row out into the ripples to see the big sun go down behind Hammerton Church. And while the boat rocked gently on the wash of tugs, he would sit motionless, trying to store the sunset in his mind. He would look at the lights in the water, the unimaginable pattern and colouring of the clouds, fretted like the sand when the sea goes out, consciously realizing, consciously memorizing, thinking, 'I must remember how that looked!' For he was not naturally observant, and often, he knew, made up for his lack of observation by his power of imagining. But the critics said he was observant, and observant he was determined to be.

Or he would row across to the eastern end of the Island and tie his boat to the single willow tree that stood there. From this point, looking eastward, you saw the whole of the splendid reach, curving magnificently away to Hammersmith Bridge. You saw the huddled, irregular houses beside it glowing golden in the last sunlight, with here and there a window that blazed at you like a furnace; you saw the fine old trees on the southern bank and the tall chimneys and the distant church that had something of the grace of Magdalen Tower, and you saw the wide and exuberant stream with an impression of bigness and dignity which could never be commanded from the bank; and you saw it rich with colour and delicate lights – with steel-blue and gold – with copper and with rose. You knew that it was a thick and muddy stream, that most of the houses were squalid houses, and many of the buildings were ugly buildings. But they were all beautiful in the late sun, and Stephen loved them.

And while he sat there, the poem hovered always in the background of his mind. Everything he saw he saw as material which might somehow take its place in the poem. Sometimes half-consciously he was shaping ahead the scheme of what he had next to do, the general form and sequence of it; and sometimes there was a line that would not come right, a word or a phrase that would not surrender itself, and this problem would be always busy in his head, the alternatives chasing each other in a tumbling perpetual circle. Sometimes he would go into the house again in a vague depression, simply because this difficulty had not yet resolved itself.

But there were certain evenings of such peace and quiet dignity that he was stricken with a brief and unwilling remorse. Then the poem was at last thrust out of his mind; then he thought of Margery and the wrong he had done her, and of John and the wrong he was doing him, and shame took hold of him. At these moments he had an impulse to abandon his plans, to forget his poem and his ambitions and his love of life, and give himself up suddenly to the police. This was usually when the sun was yet warm and wonderful. But when the sun had gone, and he had come back into the dark and silent garden, this mood departed quickly. Fear came back to him then, the love of warmth and light and comfort and life, and with that the love of praise and the desire of success. And then he would think passionately again of his poem; he would snatch, as it were in self-defence, at the pride and excitement of his purpose, and comfort his soul with new assurances of his own exceeding worth.

And when he had recaptured that consoling, invigorating mood, the great contradiction would smite him with a fresh and glorious force, the contradiction of his personal vileness and the beauty and nobility of the work which he was doing. Then as he sat down in the bright island of light at his table he would think again, with a kind of conceited malice, of the blind and stupid world which judged a man by his work – which would slobber over a murderer and a liar and a betrayer of friends simply because he could write good verse about good men.

And sometimes he even formed this thought into an arrogant phrase, 'They think they know me, the damned fools – but they don't!'

Then he would go on with the noble poem. And Margery Byrne lay silent alone in the cool bedroom, thinking of Stephen.

CHAPTER X

So the weeks went by. And John and Stephen saw little of each other. Indeed, they saw little of anyone. Then, towards the end of June, Margery Byrne got up for the first time, and little Joan came home from her grandmother's. In a week Margery was completely and delightedly 'up,' full of plans and longing to take up life exactly where she had left it. Stephen found her curiously eager for company, and especially the company of old friends; it seemed to her so long since she had seen them. Very soon she asked why John Egerton was so neglecting them. 'Get him to come round, Stephen,' she said. 'Ring him up now.' Stephen had lately told her the story of the inquest, of the local feeling and faction; and Margery had at once determined that she would think nothing of it. She would do as the Whittakers did; not that she was prepared in any case to believe evil of John. Yet at the back of her mind there was just a hint of curiosity about it.

So Stephen reluctantly rang him up – reluctantly because he had wanted to work that evening, and because he feared this meeting. But he did not dare to seem unwilling.

And John Egerton came. He had known for some days that he would soon have to do it, and he, too, had been afraid. But this evening he was almost glad of the invitation. The long weeks of semi-isolation had tried him very severely. The sense of being an outcast from his fellows, suspected, despised, had grown unreasonably and was a perpetual irritant to the nerves. He had an aching to go again into a friend's house, to

161

sit and talk again with other men. And even the house of the Byrnes and the company of the Byrnes might be a soothing relief from his present loneliness.

And now that Margery was up and well, the time was surely near when something would be done about this business. Unpleasant things had happened. The family of the Gaunts had been to see him. They had come again this evening – in the middle of supper – sly, grasping, malicious people, a decayed husband of about fifty with a drooping, ragged moustache, with watery eyes and the aspect of a wet rat, and an upright, aggressive, spiteful little wife with an antique bonnet fixed very firmly on the extreme summit of her yellowish hair. She had thin lips, a harsh voice, and an unpleasant manner. There was also a meek son of about twenty, and Emily's fiancée who looked conscientiously sad and respectable and wore a bowler hat. But the woman did all the talking. The men only interposed when they felt that she was going too far to be effective.

They wanted money. The men might be half-ashamed of wanting it, but they wanted it, and they clearly expected to get it. They assumed as common ground that John had made away with Emily and had only been preserved from arrest by the strange eccentricities of the law. They did not want trouble made, but there it was: Emily had been a good daughter to them and had contributed money to the household; and it was only fair that something should be done to heal the injury to their affections and their accounts. If not, of course, there would *have* to be trouble.

John Egerton, disgusted and humiliated, had nobly kept his temper, but firmly refused to give them a penny. They had gone away, muttering threats. John had no idea what they would do, but they filled him with loathing and fear. He could not endure this much longer for any man's sake. Stephen must release him.

But the evening at the Byrnes' house did nothing to clear things up. Rather it aggravated the tangle. Mrs Byrnes was lying on the sofa, looking more fragile yet more delicious than he had ever seen her. She greeted him very kindly and they talked for a little, while Stephen sat rather glumly in the window-seat staring out at the river.

She spoke happily of Stephen Michael Hilary Byrne, of his charm and his intelligence, and how already he really had something of Stephen about him; and as she said that she smiled at Stephen. And she leaned back with a little sigh of content and looked round at her drawing-room, rich with warm and comfortable colour, at the striped material of delicate purple, at the Japanese prints she had bought with Stephen at a sale, at the curious but excellent wallpaper of dappled grey, and the pleasant rows of books on the white shelves, at the flowers in the Chinese bowl which Stephen had bought for her in some old shop, and the mass of roses on the shiny Sheraton table; then she looked out through the window at the red light of a tug sliding mysteriously down through the steely dark and back again at Stephen. And John knew that she was counting up her happiness; and he thought with an intense pity and rage how precarious that happiness was. He realized then that he could not allow Stephen to 'do the right thing'; he would not press for it. After all, it was a small thing for himself to suffer, this petty local suspicion, even the visitations of the Gaunts, compared with the suffering which this dear and delicate lady would have to bear if the truth was told. Surely it was an easy sacrifice for a man to make.

So John sat glowing with sentiment and resolution, and Margery pondered the happiness of life, and Stephen brooded darkly in the window, and they were all silent. Then Margery suggested that the two men should sing together as they used to do; and they sang. They sang odd things from an Old English song book, picked out at random as they turned over the leaves. And it seemed as if every song in that book must have for those two some hidden and sinister meaning. It was bad enough, in any case, to stand there together behind Margery at the piano, and try to sing as they had sung in the old days, when nothing had happened. But these songs had some terrible innuendoes: 'Blow, blow, thou winter wind,' they sang first, and 'Sigh no more, ladies.' And when they came to 'a friend's ingratitude' and 'fellowship forgot' and 'Men were deceivers ever' the two men became foolishly self-conscious. They looked studiously in front of them, and each in his heart hoped that the other had not noticed, hoped that his own expression was perfectly normal and composed. It was exceedingly foolish. There were other songs like this, and after a few more Stephen said shortly that that was enough.

Then they tried to talk again; but the men could think of no topic which did not somehow lead them near to Emily Gaunt and such dangerous ground. Even when Margery began to speak of the motor-boat, then seemed to be stricken silly and dumb. Margery wondered what ailed them, till she remembered about John's 'wood-collecting' evidence, and blushed suddenly at her folly.

Stephen went down with John to the front door feeling certain that he would be there and then 'have it out.' But John said nothing, only a quick 'Good night.' He did not look at Stephen. They felt then like strangers to each other. And Stephen, marvelling at John's silence and strangely moved by his coldness, became suddenly anxious to get at his thoughts.

He said, 'John – I – I – I hope you're not ... hadn't I better ... I – I mean ... are you being worried much ... by this...?'

His vagueness was partly due to a new and genuine nervousness and partly to calculation – a half-conscious determination not to commit himself. But John perfectly understood.

'No, Stephen, we'll forget all that ... you're not to do anything... It's a bit trying, but I can stand it. I don't want to upset things any more now ... Margery and you ... a fresh start, you know... Good night.' And he was gone.

Stephen went slowly upstairs, astonished and ashamed, with a confused sense of humiliation and relief And while he felt penitent and mean in the face of this magnanimity of John's, he could not avoid a certain conceited contentment with the wisdom and success of his planning.

Yes, it was very satisfactory. And now he could get on with the poem about 'Chivalry.' He sat down at his table and pulled out the scribbled muddle of manuscript. But he wrote no word that night. He sat for a long time staring at the paper, thinking of the chivalry of John Egerton. And it brought no inspiration.

CHAPTER XI

John went home, thinking pitifully of Margery Byrne and vowing hotly that he would sacrifice himself for her sake. In the hall he found a letter from Miss Muriel Tarrant. The neat round writing on the envelope stirred him deliciously where it stared up from the floor. Almost reverently he picked it up and fingered it and turned it over and examined it with the fond and foolish deliberation of a lover for whom custom has not staled these little blisses. The letter was an invitation to a dance. The Tarrants had just come home and they were taking a party to the Buxton Galleries on Saturday. And they were very anxious for John to go. It was clear, then, that they had declined to join the faction of Mrs Vincent, though they must have heard the story, numbers of stories, by this time. And John, as he argued thus, was almost overwhelmed with pride and tenderness and exultation. He felt then that he had known always that Muriel was different from the malicious sheep who were her mother's friends. And this letter, coming at this moment, seemed like some glorious sign of approbation from

Heaven, an acknowledgment and a reward for the deed of sacrifice to which he had but just devoted himself. It was an inspiration to go on with it – though it made the sacrifice itself seem easy.

He took the letter to his bed and laid it on the table beside him. And for a long time he pondered in the dark the old vague dreams of Muriel and marriage which, since the coming of the letter, had presented themselves with such startling clearness. He had not seen her for many weeks, but this letter was like a first meeting; it was a revelation. He knew she was not clever, perhaps not even very intelligent; but she was young and lovely and kind; and she should be the simple companion of his simple heart. He was very lonely in this dark house, very silent and alone. He wanted someone who would bring voices and colour into his home, would make it a glowing and intimate place, like Margery Byrne's. Poor Margery! And Muriel would do this.

But he would have hard work to bring this about. He knew very little what she thought of him. He would be very accomplished and winning at this dance. Probably there would be four of them – Muriel and himself and her young brother George and some flame of his. They would dance together most of the evening, and he would dance with Muriel. And he must not be awkward – slide about or tread on her toes. He was not 'keen on dancing,' and he was not good at dancing. But he could 'get round'; and Muriel would teach him the rest. She loved teaching people.

But the party was to be a larger affair than John had imagined it. There were to be at least six, if the men could be found. And in the morning Muriel Tarrant came herself to the Byrnes' house and asked if Stephen would come. It was a bold suggestion, for she did not know him very well, and she knew that he seldom danced, seldom indeed 'went out' at all in the evenings. But such boldness became a virtue in the post-war code of decorum, and she was a bold person, Muriel Tarrant. This morning she looked very fresh and alluring, with her fair hair creeping in calculated abandon from a small blue hat and a cluster of tiny black feathers fastened at the side of it – tiny feathers, but somehow inexpressibly naughty. They wandered downwards over the little curls at the side of her head and nestled delicately against her face.

Margery was yet in bed, and Stephen took his visitor out into the hot garden, where little Joan was wheeling sedately a small pram and the rabbits lay panting in dark corners. And first he said that he would not go to the dance. He was busy and he did not love dancing; and anyhow Margery could not go. But Muriel perched herself in the low wall over the river, and leaned forward with her blue eyes on his, and a little pout about her lips; and she said, 'Oh, *do*, Mr Byrne.' And there was a kind of personal appeal in her voice and her eagerness and her steady smiling eyes that woke up his vanity and his admiration. He thought, 'She really thinks it is important that I should go; she likes me.' And then, 'And I like her.' And then he said that he would go. They talked a little in the sun before she went, and when she was gone Stephen felt as if some secret had passed between them. Also he wondered why he had thought so little of her existence before. And Muriel went down The Chase, smiling at some secret thought.

They dined hurriedly at Brierleys' that Saturday. Muriel and her brother and Stephen and John, and two young sisters of the name of Atholl, to whom George Tarrant owed an apparently impartial allegiance. They were equally plump and unintelligent, and neither was exciting to the outward eye, but it seemed that they danced well. But to young George this was the grand criterion of fitness for the purposes of a dance. John's idea of a dance – and Stephen's – was a social function at which you encountered pleasant people with whom, because there was dancing, one danced. But it was soon made clear to him that these were the withered memories of an obsolete age. For this was the time of the Great Craze. A dance now was no social affair; it was a semi-gladiatorial display to which one went to perform a purely physical operation with those who were physically most fitted to perform it. Dancing had passed out of the 'party' stage; it was no longer even a difficult, but agreeable and universal pastime; it was practically a profession. It was entirely impossible, except for the very highly gifted, even to approximate to the correct standards of style and manner without spending considerable sums of money on their own tuition. And when they had finished their elaborate and laborious training, and were deemed worthy to take the floor at the Buxton Galleries at all, they found that their new efficiency was a thin and ephemeral growth. The steps and rhythms and dances which they had but yesterday acquired, at how much trouble and expense, passed today into the contemptible limbo of the unfashionable, like the hats of last spring; and so the life of the devotee was one long struggle to keep himself abreast of the latest invention of the astute but commercially-minded professional teachers. 'For ever climbing up the climbing wave,' for ever studying, yet for ever out-of-date, he oscillated hopefully between the Buxton Galleries and his chosen priest; and so swift and ruthless were the changes of fashion and the whims of the priesthood, that in order to get your money's worth of the last trick you had learned, it was necessary, during its brief life of respectability, to dance at every available opportunity. You danced as many nights a week as was physically or financially possible; you danced on weekdays, and you danced on Sundays; you began dancing in the afternoon, and you danced during tea in the coffee-rooms of expensive restaurants, whirling your precarious way through littered and abandoned tea-tables; and at dinner-time you leapt up madly before the fish and danced like variety *artistes* in a highly polished arena before a crowd of complete strangers eating their food; or, as if seized with an uncontrollable craving for the dance, you flung out after the joint for one wild galop in an outer room, from which you returned, sweating and dyspeptic, to the consumption of an iced pudding, before dashing forth to the final orgy at a night-club, or a gallery, or the mansion of an earl. But it was seldom that you danced at anybody's mansion. The days of private and hospitable dances were practically dead. Nobody could afford to give as many dances as the dancing cult required. Moreover, at private dances there were old-fashioned conventions and hampering politenesses to be observed. You might have to dance occasionally out of mere courtesy with some person who was three weeks behind the times, who could not do the Jimble or the Double-Jazz Glide, or might even have an attachment for the degrading and obsolete Waltz. On the other hand, you would not be allowed to dance the entire evening with 'the one woman in the room who can do the Straddle properly,' and there was a prejudice against positive indecency. So it was better from all points of view to pay a few guineas and go to a gallery or a restaurant or a night-club with a small number of selected women, dragooned by long practice into a slavish harmony with the niceties of your particular style and favourite steps. And after all, what with the dancing lessons, and the dance-dinners, and the dance-teas, and the taxis to dances, and the taxis away from dances, and the tickets for dances, and the subscriptions to night-clubs, and the life-memberships of night-clubs which perished after two years, you had so much capital invested in the industry that you simply could not *afford* to have a moment's pleasure placed in jeopardy by deficiencies of technique in your guests. Away, then, with mere Beauty and mere Charm and mere Intelligence and mere Company! Bring out the Prize Mares and show us their steps and their stamina, their powers of endurance and harmonious submission, before we consent to appear with them in the public and costly arena.

A party selected on these lines, however suitable for the serious business of the evening, could be infinitely wearisome for the purposes of dinner. Stephen thought he had never beheld two young women so little entertaining as the two Misses Atholl. All they talked of and all that George Tarrant talked of was the dances they had been to, and were going to, and could not go to, and the comparative values of various mutual friends, considered solely as dancers. It was like the tedious 'shop' of the more fanatical golfers; and indeed at any moment Stephen expected to hear that some brave or other had a handicap of three at the Buxton Galleries, or had become stale from over-training, or ruined his form by ordinary walking. Stephen (or Muriel) had taken care that they should be sitting together, but though her talk was less restricted in range than the talk of the Atholls, Stephen began to wish intensely that he had not come. And he thought of Margery, and was sorry that he had left her alone in the house to come and listen to this futile jabbering. She had approved enthusiastically of his coming, for she thought that he went out too little; but she had looked rather wistful, he thought, when he left. She liked dancing herself.

To John, too, the talk at dinner and the personality (if any) of the Misses Atholl was inexpressibly dull; and since he was as far away from Muriel as it was possible for him to be, and since she scarcely spoke a word to anyone but Stephen, he had nothing to console him but a few provocative glances and the hope of seeing more of her at the dance. And even this hope was dimmed by the presence of Stephen and the intimidating technicalities of the conversation. He did not understand why Stephen had come, and he rather resented his coming. Wherever Stephen was one of the company, he always felt himself closing up socially like an awed anemone in the presence of a large fish. And tonight in that dominating presence he could not see in himself the brilliant and romantic figure which he had determined to be at this party. It was far from being the kind of party he had expected.

The amazing language of young George and the Misses Atholl made it still less likely that that figure could be achieved at the dance. What were these 'Rolls' and 'Buzzes' and 'Slides,' he wondered. And how did one do them? The art of dancing seemed to have acquired strange complexities since he had last attempted it eighteen months ago. Then with a faint pride he had mastered the Fox Trot and something they called a Boston. They had seemed very daring and difficult then, but already it seemed they were dead. At any rate they were never mentioned. John foresaw some hideous embarrassments, and he too wished fervently that he had not come.

But Muriel as least was enjoying herself. She was feeling unusually mischievous and irresponsible. She twinkled mischief at John's glum face, and she twinkled mischief into Stephen's eyes. Only they were two different kinds of mischief. She had long been fond of John 'in a kind of way'; she was still fond of him 'in a kind of way.' But he was a slow and indefinite suitor, old John, and he was undeniably not exciting. However, there was no one she liked better, and if he should ever bring himself to the pitch of suggesting it, she had little doubt that she would take him. His income would not be large, but it would be certain.

But it was slow work waiting, and this evening she had Stephen Byrne; and Stephen Byrne was undeniably exciting. Not simply because he was a great poet, – for though she liked 'poitry' in a vague way, she did not like any one poet or one piece of poetry much better than another – but because he had made a *success* of poetry, a worldly success. He had made a name, he had even made money; he was a well-known man. And he was handsome and young, and his hair was black, and that morning in the garden he had admired her. She knew that. And she knew that she had touched his vanity by her urgency and his senses by her charm, and something naughty had stirred in her, and that too he had seen and enjoyed with a sympathetic naughtiness. And she had thought to herself that it would be an amusing thing to captivate this famous young man, this married, respectable, delightful youth; it would be interesting to see how powerful she could be. And at least she might waken John Egerton into activity.

They went on to the dance in two taxis. John found himself on one of the small seats with his back to the driver, with Stephen and Muriel chattering aloofly together in the gloom of the larger seat. The small seat in a taxi is, at the best of times, a position of moral and strategic inferiority, and tonight John felt this keenly. He screwed his head round uncomfortably in his sharp collar and pretended to be profoundly interested in the wet and hurrying streets. But he heard every word they said; and they said no word to him.

From the door of the galleries where the dancing was done, a confused uproar overflowed into the passages, as if several men of powerful physique were banging a number of pokers against a number of saucepans, and blowing whistles, and occasional cat-calls, and now and then beating a drum and

177

several sets of huge cymbals, and ceaselessly twanging at innumerable banjos, and at the same time singing in a foreign language, and shouting curses or exhortations or street-cries, or imitating hunting-calls or the cry of the hyena, or uniting suddenly in the final warwhoop of some pitiless Indian tribe. It was a really terrible noise. It hit you like the breath of an explosion as you entered the room. There was no distinguishable tune. It was simply an enormous noise. But there was a kind of savage rhythm about it, which made John think immediately of Indians and fierce men and the native camps which he had visited at the Earl's Court Exhibition. And this was not surprising; for the musicians included one genuine Negro and three men with their faces blacked; and the noise and the rhythm were the authentic music of a Negro village in South America; and the words which some genius had once set to the noise were an exhortation to go to the place where the Negroes dwelt.

To judge by their movements, John thought, many of the dancers had in fact been there, and carefully studied the best indigenous models. They were doing some quite extraordinary things. No two couples were doing quite the same thing for more than a few seconds; so that there was an endless variety of extraordinary motions and extraordinary postures. Some of them shuffled secretly along the edge of the room, their faces tense, their shoulders swaying faintly like reeds in a light wind, their progress almost imperceptible; they did not rotate, they did not speak, but sometimes the tremor of a skirt or the slight stirring of a patent leather shoe showed that they were indeed alive and in motion, though that motion was as the motion of a glacier not to be measured in minutes or yards. And some, in a kind of fever, rushed hither and thither among the thick crowd, avoiding disaster with marvellous dexterity; and sometimes they revolved slowly and sometimes quickly, and sometimes spun giddily round for a moment like gyroscopic tops. Then they too would be seized with a kind of trance, or, it may be, with sheer shortness of breath, and hung motionless for a little in the centre of the room, while the mad throng jostled and flowed about them like leaves in autumn round a dead bird. And some did not revolve at all, but charged straightly up and down; and some of these thrust their loves for ever before them, as the Prussians thrust the villagers in the face of the enemy, and some for ever navigated themselves backwards like moving breakwaters to protect their darlings from the rough seas of tangled women and precipitate men. Some of them kept themselves as upright as possible, swaying gracefully like willows from the hips, and some of them contorted themselves into hideous and angular shapes, now leaning perilously forward till they were practically lying upon their terrified partners, and now bending sideways as a man bends who has water in one ear after bathing. All of them clutched each other in a close and intimate manner, but some, as if by separation to intensify the joy of their union, or perhaps to secure greater freedom for some particularly spacious manoeuvre, would part suddenly in the middle of the room and, clinging distantly with their hands, execute a number of complicated sidesteps in opposite directions, or aim a series of vicious kicks at each other, after which they would reunite in a passionate embrace, and gallop in a frenzy round the room, or fall into a trance, or simply fall down; if they fell down they lay still for a moment in the fearful expectation of death, as men lie who fall under a horse: and then they would creep on hands and knees to the shore through the mobile and indifferent crowd.

Watching them you could not tell what any one couple would do next. The most placid and dignified among them might at any moment fling a leg out behind them and almost kneel in mutual adoration, and then, as if nothing unusual had happened, shuffle solemnly onward through the press; or, as

180

though some electric mechanism had been set in motion, they would suddenly lift a foot sideways and stand on one leg, reminding the observer irresistibly of a dog out for a walk; or, with the suggestion of an acrobat nerving himself for the final effort of daring, the male would plant himself firmly on both feet while his maiden laboriously leapt a half-circle through the air about the tense figure of her swain. It was marvellous with what unanimity these eccentricities were performed. So marvellous, John thought, that it was impossible to think of them as spontaneous, joyous expressions of art. He imagined the male issuing his orders during the long minutes of shuffling motion, carefully manoeuvring into position, sizing up like a general the strategic situation, and then hoarsely whispering the final 'Now!' And after that they moved on with all the nonchalance of extreme self-consciousness, thinking, no doubt, 'It cost me a lot to learn that – but it was worth it.'

The look of their faces confirmed this view, for nearly all were set and purposeful and strained, as men who have serious work in hand; not soulful, not tense with emotion, but simply expressive of concentration. With few exceptions there was nothing of the joy of life in those faces, the rapture of music or of motion. They meant business. And this was the only thing that could absolve many of them from the charge of public indecency; for it was clear that their motions and the manner of their embraces were not the expression of licence or affection so much as matters of technique.

Upon this whirlpool John Egerton embarked with the gravest misgivings, especially as he was conscious of a strange Miss Atholl clinging to his person. Young George Tarrant had immediately plunged into the storm with her sister, and his fair head was to be seen far off, gleaming and motionless like a lighthouse above the tossing heads and undulant shoulders. Stephen had secured Muriel Tarrant, and poor John was very miserable. If he had been less shy, or more intimate with Miss Atholl, be might have comforted himself with the comedy of it all. And if he had been more ruthless he might have bent Miss Atholl to his will and declined to attempt anything but his own primitive two-step. But he became solemn and panic-stricken, and surrendered his hegemony to her, suffering her to give him intricate advice in a language which was meaningless to him, and to direct him with ineffectual tugs and pushes which only made his bewilderment worse. The noise was deafening, the atmosphere stifling, the floor incredibly slippery. The four black men were now all shouting at once, and playing all their instruments at once, working up to the inconceivable uproar of the finale, and all the dancers began to dance with a last desperate fury and velocity. Bodies buffeted John from behind, and while he was yet looking round in apology or anger, other bodies buffeted him from the flank, and more bodies buffeted his partner and pressed her against his reluctant frame. It was like swimming in a choppy sea, where there is no time to recover from the slap and buffets of one wave before the next one smites you.

Miss Atholl whispered, 'Hold me tighter,' and John, blushing faintly at these unnatural advances, tightened a little his ineffectual grip. The result of this was that he kicked her more often on the ankle and trod more often on her toes. Close beside him a couple fell down with a crash and a curse and the harsh tearing of satin. John glanced at them in concern, but was swept swiftly onward with the tide. He was dimly aware now that the black men were standing on their chairs bellowing, and fancied the end must be near. And with this thought he found himself surprisingly in a quiet backwater, a corner between two rows of chairs, from which he determined never to issue till the Last Banjo should indeed sound. And here he sidled and shuffled vaguely for a little, hoping that he gave the impression of a man preparing himself for some vast culminating feat, a sidestep, or a 'buzz,' or a double-Jazz-spin, or whatever these wonders might be.

Then the noise suddenly ceased; there was a burst of perfunctory clapping, and the company became conscious of the sweat of their bodies. John looked round longingly for Muriel.

But Muriel was happily chattering to Stephen Byrne in a deep sofa surrounded by palms. Stephen, like John, had surveyed the new dancing with dismay, but his dismay was more artistic than personal. He was as much amused as disguised, and he did not intend, for any woman, to make himself ridiculous by attempting any of the more recent monstrosities.

But, unlike John, he had the natural spirit of dancing in his soul; so that he was able to ignore the freakish stupidities of the scene, and extract an artistic elemental pleasure of his own from the light and the colour and excitement, from the barbaric rhythm of the noise and the seductive contact of Muriel Tarrant. So he took her and swung her defiantly round in an ordinary old-fashioned waltz; and she, because it was the great Stephen Byrne, felt no shame at this sacrilege.

When they had come to the sofa, she talked for a little the idle foolishness which is somehow inseparable from the intervals between dances, and he thought, 'I wonder whether she always talks like this. I wonder if she reads my poems. I wonder if she likes them.' He began to wish that she would pay him a compliment about them, even an unintelligent compliment. It might jar upon him intellectually, but, coming from her, it would still be pleasing. For it is a mistake to suppose that great artists are so remote from the weaknesses of other men that they are not sometimes ready to have their vanity tickled by a charming girl at the expense of their professional sensibilities.

But she only said, 'It's a ripping band here. I hope you'll come here again, Mr Byrne.' And he thought, 'What a conversation!' How could one live permanently with a conversation like this? But old John could!

But as she said it she looked him in the eyes very directly and delightfully, and once again there was the sense of a secret passing between them.

Then they went to look for John, and Muriel determined that she would be very nice to him. The next dance was, nominally, a waltz, and that was a rare event. John asked if he might waltz in the ancient fashion, and though she was being con-scientiously sweet and gracious to him, and though she had made no murmur when Stephen had done as John would like to do, some devil within her made her refuse. She said that he must do the Hesitation Waltz as other people were doing. The chief point of this seemed to be that you imitated the dog, not by spasms, but consistently. Even the most expert practitioner failed to invest this feat with elegance and dignity, and the remainder, poising themselves pathetically with one leg in the air, as if waiting for the happy signal when they might put it down, would have looked ridiculous if they had not looked so sad. Stephen, revolving wearily with the younger Miss Atholl, wished that the Medusa's head might be smuggled into the room for the attitudes of this dance to be imperishably recorded in cold stone. Then he caught sight of the unhappy John, and was smitten with an amused sympathy. John's study of the habits of dogs had evidently been superficial, and he did not greatly enjoy his first dance with his love. He held her very reverently and loosely, though dimly aware that this made things much more difficult, but he could not bring himself to seize that soft and altogether sacred form in the kind of intimate clutch which the other men affected – Stephen, he noticed, included. It was a maddening complexity of emotion, that dance – the incredible awe and rapture of holding his adored, however lightly, in his arms, the intoxication of her nearness, the fragrance of her dress, and the touch of her hair upon his face – and all this ruined by the exasperating futility of the actual dance, the vile necessity of thinking whether he was in time with the music and in time with Muriel, and if he was going to run into the couple ahead, and if there was room to reverse in that corner, and whether he should cock his leg up farther, or not so far, or not at all. He envied bitterly the easy accomplishment of the circling youths about him, who, for all the earnestness of their expressions, had each of them, no doubt, time to appreciate the fact that they held on their arms some warm and lovely girl.

Yet Muriel was very kind and forbearing and instructive, and at the end of it he did feel that he had made some progress, both with his hesitating and his suit. They sat in the interval on the same sofa, and Muriel was still gracious. She told him that he would pick it up very quickly, that it was all knack, that it was all balance, that it was all practice, that no practice was needed. And John believed everything and was much excited and pleased. He thanked her for her advice, and vowed that he would take lessons and become expert. And Muriel thought, 'He will never be able to dance; could I live permanently with a man like that?' She thought what a prim, funny 'old boy' he was. But he was a nice 'old boy,' and that rumour about the maid-servant was positively ridiculous.

The next dance she had promised to Stephen. The four black men were playing a wild and precipitate tune. A certain melody was distinguishable, and it had less of the lunacies of extravagant syncopation than most of their repertoire. But it was a wicked tune, a hot, provocative, passionate tune, that fired a man with a kind of fever of motion. Faster and faster, and louder and louder, the black men played; and though it was impossible for the dancers to move much faster because of the press, their entranced souls responded to the gathering urgency of the music, and they clutched their partners more tightly, and they were conscious no more of the sweat upon their bodies, of their sore toes, or disordered dresses, they forgot for a moment the technical details of the movements of their feet, and they were whirled helplessly on in a savage crescendo of noise and motion and physical rapture towards the final Elysium of licence to which this dance must surely lead them.

Stephen Byrne felt the fever and enjoyed it. He enjoyed it equally as a personal indulgence and as an artistic experience. He held Muriel very close, and found himself dancing with an eager pleasure which surprised him. Yet as he danced, he was noticing his own sensations and the faces of the people about him, the intense faces of the men, the drugged expressions of the women. He saw oldish men looking horribly young in their animal excitement, and oldish women looking horrible in their coquettishness. And he saw them all as literary material. He thought, 'This is good copy.'

Muriel, he knew, was enjoying it too. Her eyes were half-closed, her face, a little pale, had the aspect of absolute surrender which can be seen in churches. But sometimes she opened her eyes wide and smiled at Stephen. And this excited him very much, so that he watched for it; and when she saw that she blushed. Then he was swept with a hot gust of feeling, and he realized that he was dangerously attracted by this girl. He thought of Margery and the late vows he had made, and he was ashamed. But the mad dance went on, with ever-increasing fury, and the black men returned with a vast tempestuous chord and a shattering crash of cymbals to the original melody, and all those men and women braced themselves to snatch the last moment of this intoxication. Those who were dancing with bad partners or dull partners were filled with bitterness because they were not getting the full measure of the dance; and those who held the perfect partners in their arms, foresaw with sorrow the near end of their rapture, and began, if they had not already begun, to conceive for each other a certain sentimental regard. Stephen thought no more of Margery, but he thought tenderly of Muriel and the moment when the dance must end. For when it ended all would be over; he might not hold her in his arms any more, he might not enjoy her loveliness in any way, because he was married, and she was dedicated to John. She was too good for John. But because he was married he must stand aside and see her sacrificed to John or to somebody like John. He must not interfere with that. But he would like to interfere. He would like to kiss her at the end of the dance.

The dance was finished at last, and while they sat together afterwards, hot and exhausted, Muriel said suddenly, 'What's all this about Mr Egerton – and – that maid of yours–? There are some horrid stories going round – Mrs Vincent – Mother said she wouldn't listen to any of them.'

Stephen was silent for a little. Then he said, in a doubtful, deliberate manner:

'Well, I've known John as long as anybody in The Chase, and I know he's a jolly good fellow, but – but– It was an extraordinary affair, that, altogether. I don't know what to make of it.' He finished with a sigh of perplexity.

Then he sat silent again, marvelling at himself, and Muriel said no more.

John came up and stood awkwardly before

them. He wanted to ask Muriel for the next dance, but he was too shy to begin. His dress-suit was ill-fitting and old, his hair ruffled, his tie crooked, and as she lay back on the sofa Muriel could see a glimpse of shirt between the top of his trousers and the bottom of the shrunken and dingy white waistcoat, where any pronounced movement of his body caused a spasmodic but definite hiatus. His shirt front had buckled into a wide dent. Of all these things poor John was acutely conscious as he stood uncertainly before the two.

Stephen said heartily, 'Hallo, old John, you look a bit the worse for wear. How did you get on that time?'

John stammered, 'Not very well – I want Miss Tarrant to give me some more – some more instruction.' And he looked at Muriel, an appealing, pathetic look. He wished very fiercely that Stephen was not there – so easy and dashing, and certain of himself

And Muriel had no smile for him. She glanced inquiringly at Stephen, and said, with the hard face of a statue, 'I'm sorry, I'm doing the next with Mr Byrne.' And Stephen nodded.

She danced no more with John that night. Sometimes as he sat out disconsolately with one of the Atholl women, she brushed him with her skirt, or he saw her distantly among the crowd. And he looked now with a new longing at the adorable poise of her head upon her shoulders, at the sheen and texture of her hair, at the grace and lightness of her movements, as she swam past with Stephen. He looked after her till she was lost in the press, trying to catch her eye, hoping that she might see him and smile at him. But if she saw him she never smiled. And when he was sick with love and sadness, and hated the Atholls with a bitter hatred, he left the building alone, and went home miserably by the Underground.

CHAPTER XII

July drew on to a sultry end. In the little gardens of Hammerton the thin lawns grew yellow and bare: and there, by the river-wall, the people of The Chase took their teas and their suppers, and rested gratefully in the evening cool. One week after the dance the Byrnes were to go away into the country, and Margery had looked forward eagerly to the 27th of July. But Stephen said on the 25th that he could not come: he had nearly finished the poem 'Chivalry,' and he wanted to finish it before he went away; and he had much business to settle with publishers and so on: he was publishing a volume of

Collected Poems, and there were questions of type and paper and cover to be determined; and he had a long article for *The Epoch* to do. All these things might take a week or they might take a fortnight; but he would follow Margery as soon as he might – she could feel sure of that.

Against this portentous aggregate of excuses Margery argued gently and sorrowfully but vainly. And sorrowfully she went away with Nurse and Joan and Michael Hilary. She went away to Hampshire, to the house of an old friend – a lovely place on the shore of the Solent. You drove there from Brockenhurst through the fringes of the New Forest, through marvellous regiments of ancient trees, and wild stretches of heathery waste, and startling patches of hedge and pasture, where villages with splendid names lurked slyly in unexpected hollows, and cows stood sleepily by the rich banks of little brooks. And when you came to the house, you saw suddenly the deep blue band of the Solent, coloured like the Dardanelles, and quiet like a lake. Beyond it rose the green foothills of the Island, patched with the brown of ploughlands and landslides by the sea, and far-off the faint outline of Mottistone Down and Brighstone Down, little heights that had the colour and dignity of great mountains when the light caught them in the early morning or in the evening or after the rain. On the water small white boats with red sails and green sails shot about like butterflies, and small black fishing-craft prowled methodically near the shore. And sometimes in the evening a great liner stole out of Southampton Water and crept enormously along the farther shore, her hull a beautiful grey, her funnel an indescribable tint, that was neither pink nor scarlet nor red, but fitted perfectly in the bright picture of the land and the sea. And all day there were ships passing, battleships and aged tramps and dredgers and destroyers, and sometimes a tall sailing-ship that looked like an old engraving, and big yachts with sails like snow, and little yachts with sails like cinnamon or the skin of an Arab boy. At low tide there were long stretches of mud-flats and irregular pools, before the house and far away to the west; and these at sunset were places of great beauty. For the sunset colours of the tumbled clouds, and the subtle green of the lower sky and the bold blue of the cloudless spaces above were in these pools and in the near shallows of the sea perfectly recaptured. In this delicate mosaic of golden pools and rose pools and nameless lights herons moved with a majestic stealth or stood like ebony images, watching for fish; and little companies of swans swam up and down with the arrogant beauty of all swans and the unique beauty of swans in sea water: and all the sea-birds of England circled and swooped against the sun or clustered chattering on the purple mud and saffron patches of sand, with a strange quietness, as if they, too, must do their reverence to the stillness and the splendour of that hour.

The sun went down and all those colours departed, but for a sad glow over Dorsetshire and the deep green of the Needles Light that shot along the still surface almost to your feet as you stood in the thick grass above the shore.

Then you went with the sensation of awe into the house; and the house was old and comforting and spacious, with a mellow roof of gentle red; and it was rich with the timber of Hampshire trees. There was a lawn in front of it and a tangled screen of low shrubs and sallow trees; and when Margery stood in the wide window of her room there was nothing but these between herself and the sea; and there was no building to be seen nor the work of any man, only the friendly ships and their lights, and the far smoke of a farm upon the Island, and at night the blinking lamp of a buoy-light in the Channel. To Margery it would have been the perfect haven of contentment and rest – if Stephen had come with her. But he had not come. At night the curlews flew past the windows with the long and sweet and musical cry which no other bird can utter and no man imitate, nor even interpret – for who can say from the sound of it if it be a cry of melancholy or a song of hope or rejoicing or love? But to Margery in those weeks it was a song of absolute sadness, of lost possibilities and shattered dreams, and it was the very voice of her disappointment, her protest against the exquisite tantalization of her coming to this exquisite retreat – and coming alone.

And Stephen in London worked on at 'Chivalry.' He was beginning to be tired of it now as the end of it came in sight, and it was true that he wanted to be able to leave the whole burden of it behind him when he went away. But that was not the whole reason of his staying at home, and what the whole reason was he had not consciously determined; but faintly he knew that Muriel Tarrant was part of it.

He was tired of the poem now, and was eager to be done – eager to be done with the long labour of execution of an idea no longer fresh with the first fury of inspiration. And now that so much was achieved he was urgent to finish it quickly and give it to the world, lest some other be before him. For poets and all authors suffer something of the terrors of inventors and scientific creators, toiling feverishly at the latest child of their imagination, while who knows what other man may not already have stolen their darling, may not this very hour be hurrying to the Patent Office, filching rights and the patronage of rich men, ruining perhaps for ever by their folly or avarice or imperfection the whole glory of the conception.

Stephen had this sort of secret fear. They seemed so obvious now, his idea and his scheme of execution, though at their birth they had seemed so strange and bold and original. Surely some other man had long since thought of writing a poem like his, was even now correcting his proofs, some mean and barren artist who could never do justice to the theme, but would make it for ever a stale and tawdry thing. Or maybe in the winter there would be a paper shortage or a printers' strike or a revolution, and if his masterpiece had not seen the light by then it would never see the light at all; or at best there would be long months of intolerable waiting, and it would be given to the world at the wrong season, when the world was no longer inspired with the sense of chivalry, when the critics were bored with chivalry, at Christmas time when men looked for lighter fare, or in the spring, when men wanted nothing but the spring.

So all that August he worked, thinking little of Margery, thinking little of anyone. But though there was this fever of purpose and anxiety driving him on, day by day the labour grew more wearisome and difficult. Men who go out to offices or factories to do their work think enviously sometimes of the gentler lot of the author, bound by no regulations or hours or personal entanglements, but able to sit down at his own time at his own desk and put down without physical labour or nervous strain the easy promptings of his brain. They do not know with how much terror and distaste he may have to drag himself to that desk, with what agony of mind he sits there. The nervous weariness of writing, the physical weariness of writing, the mental incubus of a great conception that must be carried unformed in the heavy mind month after weary month, for ever growing and swelling and bursting to be born, yet not able to be born, because this labour of writing is so long, the hideous labour of writing and rewriting and correcting, of futile erasions and vacillations and doubt, of endless worryings over little words and tragic sacrifices and fresh starts and rearrangements – these are terrible things. An author is to his work as a rejected lover his love, for ever drawn yet for ever repelled. Stephen sometimes in the morning would almost long to be transformed into a clerk, or a railway porter, some one who need ask little of himself since little is asked of him but the simple observance of a routine; he would have to force himself to sit on at his work, as a man forces himself to face danger or bear pain; he would even welcome interruptions, yet bitterly resent them; for when the words would not come or would not arrange themselves, when nothing went absolutely right, any distraction was sweet which legitimately for a single hour released him from the drudgery of thought; and yet it was hateful, for it postponed yet another hour the end of that drudgery, and in that precious hour – who knows? – the divine ease and assurance might have returned, the maddening difficulties melted away, so strange and fitful are the springs of inspiration.

So all these weeks he worked and saw nobody; he did not see Muriel, though the Tarrants were still at home, and he did not see John, who had gone away to Devonshire with a fellow Civil Servant. But at last in the third week the labour was finished. It was finished at sunset on a breathless evening; he finished it with a glowing sense of contentment with good work done. Then he read it over, from beginning to end. And as he read the glow faded, the contentment departed. The mournful disillusion of achievement began. Here and there were phrases which stirred, passages which satisfied; but for the most part he read his work with a sort of sick shame and disappointment. Who in the wide world could read these stale and wearisome lines? Each of them at one time had seemed the fresh and perfect expression of a fine thought; each of them was the final choice of numberless alternatives; but so often he had read them, so often written them, so often in his head endlessly recited them, in the streets and on the river or in the dark night, that they were all old now, old and dull.

He had learned by long experience to discount a little this gloomy and inevitable reaction, and now as he turned over the final page of spidery manuscript, he tried hard to restore his faith, reminding himself that the world would see his work as he saw it first himself, and not as he saw it now. Anyhow, it was done, and could not be mended any more. Perhaps it would be better when it was typed. But then the drudgery would begin again – the reading and rereading and alteration and doubt, the weary numbering of pages, the weary correction of typist's lunacies. And after that there would be proofs and the correcting of proofs; then new doubts would discover themselves, and the old doubts would live again; and he would hate it. Yet it would be better then – it would be better in print. Now he was tired of it and would forget it. He felt the impulse to relaxation and indulgence and rest which drives athletes to excesses when their race is run, their long discipline over. He went out into the garden and into the boat, and paddled gently up-stream with the tide, under the bank. It was nearly ten and the sun was long down. There was no moon and it was dark on the river with the brilliant darkness of a starry night. He paddled gently past John's house, scarcely moving the oars; past Mr Farraday's and the two moored barges at the Bakery wharf. He drifted under the fig-tree by the Whittakers', and came near to the house of the Tarrants. The Tarrant's house, like his own, was on the river side of the road, and their garden ran down to a low wall over the water. As he came out from under the fig-tree he looked up over his shoulder at the house; and Muriel Tarrant was in his mind. There was a figure in a white dress leaning motionless over the wall, and as he looked up the figure stirred sharply. Then he began to tremble with a curious excitement, for he saw that it was Muriel herself He dipped the oars in the water and stopped the boat under the wall.

She said, very softly, 'Mr Byrne?'

He said, 'Muriel,' and his voice was no more than a whisper. But she heard.

Then there was an intolerable silence, and they stared at each other through the gloom; and nothing moved anywhere but the smooth hurrying water chuckling faintly round the boat and against the oars and along the wall. They were silent, and their hearts beat with a guilty urgency; and in the thoughts of both was the same riot of doubt and scruple and exquisite excitement.

Stephen said at last, – and in his voice there was again that stealthy hoarseness, – 'Come out in the boat!'

She hesitated. She looked quickly over her shoulder at the house, which was quite dark, because her mother and their only servant had gone early to bed. Then without a word she came down the steps. She gave him a hot hand that quivered in his as he helped her down. Quietly he pushed off the boat; but on the Island a swan heard them and flew away with a startling clatter, looking very large against the stars. Still in silence they drifted away under the trees past the Tathams' and past the brewery, and past the Petways' and the ferry and the church. There was something in this silence very suggestive of wrong, making them already confessed conspirators. Muriel somehow felt this, and said at last: 'Mother's gone to bed. I mustn't be long.'

Her voice and her words and her low delightful laugh broke the spell of self-conscious wickedness which had held them. They felt at last that they really were in this boat with each other under the stars; it was no fantastic dream but an amusing and, after all, quite ordinary adventure, nothing to be ashamed of or furtive about – a gentleman and a lady boating in the evening on the Thames.

So Stephen steered out into mid-stream and pulled more strongly now, away past the empty meadows, and the first low houses of Barnes, and under the big black bridge, and round the bend by the silent factories. Then there were a few last houses, very old and dignified, and you came out suddenly into a wide reach where there moved against the stars a long procession of old elms, and the banks were clothed with an endless tangle of willows and young shrubs, drooping and dipping in the water. The tide lapped among thick reeds, and there was no murmur of London to be heard, and no houses to be seen nor the lights of houses. It was a corner of startling solitude, forgotten somehow in the urge of civilization; as if none had had the heart to build a factory there or a brewery or a wharf, but had built them resolutely to the east or to the west and all around, determined, if they could, to spare this little relic of the old country Thames.

And here Stephen stopped rowing, and tied the boat to a willow branch; and Muriel watched him, saying nothing. Then he sat down beside her in the wide stern-seat. She turned her head and looked at him, very pale against the trees. And he put his arm about her and kissed her.

It was very hot in that quiet place, and the night lay over them like a velvet covering, heavy and sensuous and still. In each of them there was the sense that this had been inevitable. They had known that it must happen in that breathless moment at the garden wall. And this was somehow comforting to the conscience.

So they sat there for a little longer, clinging tremorously in an ecstacy of passion. A tug thrashed by; there was a sudden tumult of splashing in the willows and in the reeds and the boat rocked violently against the branches. Stephen fended her off

Then they sat whispering and looking at the stars. It was a clear and wonderful sky and no star was missing. Stephen told her the names of stars and the stories about them. And she murmured dreamily that she saw and understood; but she saw nothing and understood nothing but the marvellous completeness of her conquest of this man, and the frightening completeness of his conquest of her. She had never meant that things should go so far.

And he, as he looked at the stars and the freckled gleam upon the waters and the hot white face of the girl at his side, thought also, 'I did not mean it to go so far. But it is romance, this – it is poetry, and rich experience – so it is justified.' And what he meant was, 'It is copy.'

The tide turned at last, and they drifted softly and luxuriously down to Hammerton

Reach, and stole at midnight under the hushed gardens of The Chase to the Tarrants' wall. And there again they kissed upon the steps. He whispered hotly, 'Tomorrow!' and she whispered, 'Yes – if I can–' and was gone.

In the morning there came a letter from Margery, beseeching him to come to her as soon as he could – a pathetic, gentle little letter. She drew a picture of the peace and beauty of the place, and ended acutely by emphasizing its possibilities as an inspiration to poetry.

'Do come down, my darling, as soon as you can. I do want you to be here with me for a bit. I know you want to finish the poem, but this is such a heavenly place, I'm sure it would help you to finish it; I sometimes feel like writing poetry myself here! Joan says that Daddy *must* come quick!'

Stephen wrote back, with a bewildered wonder at himself that he had nearly finished, but could not get away for at least a week. That day he wrote a love-song – dedicated 'To M.' He had never written anything of the kind before, and it excited him as nothing in 'Chivalry' had ever excited him.

All that week the tide was high in the evenings, and on the third day the moon began. And every night, when all Hammerton had gone to their early beds, he paddled secretly to the Tarrants' steps, still drunk with amorous excitement and the sense of stealthy adventure. Every night Muriel was waiting on the wall, slim and tremulous and pale; and they slipped away under the bank to the open spaces where none could see. And each day they said to themselves that this must be the last evening, for disaster must surely come of these meetings and these kisses; and each day looked forward with a hot expectancy to the evening that was to come, that must be the end of this delicious madness. Yet every night he whispered, 'Tomorrow?' and every night she whispered, 'If I can.' And each day he wrote a new love-song – dedicated 'To M.'

On the seventh day young George came down to see his sister, and, greatly daring, Stephen proposed a long expedition down the river in his motor-boat. So those three set out at noon and travelled down river in the noisy boat through the whole of London. They saw the heart of London as it can only be seen from London's river, the beauty of Westminster from Vauxhall and the beauty of the City from Westminster. And as a man walks eastward through Aldgate into a different world, they left behind them the sleek dignity of Parliament and the Temple and the Embankment and shot under Blackfriars Bridge into a different world – a world of clustering untidy bridges and sheer warehouses and endless wharves. They felt very small in the little boat that spun sideways in the bewildering eddies round the bridges and was pulled under them at breathless speed by the confined and tremendous tide. They came through London Bridge into a heavy sea, where the boat pitched and wallowed and tossed her head and plunged suddenly with frightening violence in the large waves that ran not one way only but rolled back obliquely from the massed barges by the banks, and dashed at each other and made a tumult of water, very difficult for a small boat to weather. Tugs dashed up and down and across the river with the disquieting quickness and inconsequence of taxi-cabs in the narrow space between the barges and the big steamers huddled against the wharves. The men in them looked out and laughed at the puny white boat plunging sideways under Tower Bridge. There was then an ocean-going steamer moving portentously out, and Muriel was frightened by the size of the ship, and the noise and racket of the wharves, and the hooting tugs, and the mad water splashing and heaving about them. But they came soon past Wapping into a wide and quieter reach; and here there were many ships and many barges, some anchored and some slowly moving, like ships in a dream. All of them were bright with colour against the sky and against the steel-blue water and the towering muddle of wharves and tall chimneys and warehouses upon the banks. The sails of the barges stood out far off in lovely patches of warm brown, and their masts shone like copper in the sun. Tucked away among the wharves and cranes were old, mysterious houses, with balconies and lady-like windows looking incongruously over coal-barges.

But it was all mysterious and all beautiful, Stephen thought, in this sunny market of the Thames. He liked the strange old names of the places they passed, and told them lovingly to Muriel – Limehouse Causeway, and Wapping Old Stairs, and Shadwell Basin, and Cherry Garden Pier; and he loved to see through inlets here and there the high forests of masts, and know that yonder were the special mysteries of great docks; for, for such things he had the romantic reverence of a boy. But Muriel saw no romance and little beauty in the Pool of London, and her brother George saw less. She saw it only as a strange muddle of dirty vessels and ugly buildings, strongly suggestive of slums and the East End. It was noisy sometimes, and she had been splashed with water which she knew was dirty and probably infected; she felt that she preferred the westward stretches of the Thames, where navigation was less anxious and Stephen was not so preoccupied with his surroundings.

Stephen perceived this and was aware of a faint disappointment. Only when they rounded a bend and saw suddenly the gleaming pile of Greenwich Hospital, brilliant against the green hill behind, did Muriel definitely admire. And then, Stephen thought; it was not because she saw that the building was so beautiful from that angle and in that light, but because it had such an air of cleanliness and austere respectability after the orgy of raffish and commercial scenery which she had been compelled to endure. Or perhaps it was because at Greenwich Pier they were going to get out of the boat.

CHAPTER XIII

They came home in the gathering dusk on the young flood. And because it was Saturday evening they had the river to themselves, and moved almost alone through the silent and deserted Pool. They followed slowly after the sun, and saw the Tower Bridge as a black scaffolding framing the last glow of yellow and gold. All the undiscovered colours of sunset and half-darkness lay upon the water, smooth now and velvety, and they fled away in the front of the boat as the glow departed. At Blackfriars the moon had not yet come, and Nature had made thick darkness; but man had made a marvel of light and beauty upon the water that left Stephen silent with wonder. The high trams swam along the Embankment, palaces of light, and they swam yet more admirably in the water. There were the scattered lights of the houses, and the brilliant lights of theatres, and the opulent lights of hotels, and the regimented lights of street-lamps, and the sudden little lights of matches on the banks, and the tiny lights of cigarettes, where men hung smoking on the Embankment wall, and sometimes a bright, inexplicable light high up among the roofs; and the lights of Parliament, and at last the light of the young moon peeping shyly over a Lambeth brewery – and all these lights were different and beautiful in the dark, and made a glory of the muddy water. The small boat travelled on in the lonely darkness of mid-stream, and to Stephen it seemed a wonderful thing that no other but he and Muriel and her brother George could look as they could upon those magical lights and the magical patterns that the water made of them. He had a sense of remoteness, of privileged remoteness from the world: yet he had a yearning for pleasant companionship, and itched for the moment when young George was to leave them to go to his Club.

Young George left them at Westminster Pier, and those two went on together in the boat. The lights of Chelsea were as beautiful as the lights of Westminster, and Stephen thought suddenly of Margery's description of evening by the Solent. It was hardly necessary to go so far for loveliness, he thought. He was glad that Muriel was with him, because she was too lovely, but when she clung to him in the old passionate way he kissed her very gently and without fire. For the poetry of all that he had seen that day had somehow purged him of the extravagant fever of the previous nights; and he imagined, unreasonably, that she too would be ready for this refinement of their relations. But she was not. She was tired with the long day, with trying to share an enthusiasm which she did not understand, for colours which she did not see, and lights which after all were only ordinary lights she saw in the streets on the way to dances; she wanted to have done with that kind of thing now that they were alone again; she wanted to be hotly embraced and hotly kissed. For the end of this adventure was terribly near now. After tomorrow her brother was coming to live at home again; after that there would be no more safety. Tomorrow would be the last night.

Of all this Stephen was but vaguely sensible. She was still a sweet and adorable companion, and his soul was still bursting with poetry and romance but it was the poetry of the moonlit Thames rather than the poetry of furtive passion. And because of this, and because he was dimly conscious that she looked for some more violent demonstration than he was able in the flesh to give, he thought suddenly of the Love-Songs which he had made to her, but never mentioned: and he wondered if they would please her. He stopped the engine and let the boat drift. Then, very softly, in a voice timid at first with self-consciousness, but gathering body and feeling as he went on, he spoke for her the words of his Love-Song. At the end he felt that they were very good, better than he had thought, and waited anxiously to hear what she would say. And she listened in bewilderment. She was flattered in her vanity that a poet should have written them for her; but she did not understand them, and she was not moved or deeply interested.

She said at last: 'How *nice*, Stephen! Did you really make up all that about me?'

And at that the last flicker of the fire which had burned in him for so many days went out. He saw clearly for the first time the insane unfitness of their intimacy. In the first fascination of his senses, in the voluptuous secrecy of their meetings under the moon, he had asked nothing of her intellect; he had been content with the touch of her hands, with the warm seduction of her kisses. And these, too, were still precious, but they were not enough. They were not enough to a poet on a night of poetry now that his senses were almost satisfied.

So all the way home he held her gently and talked to her tenderly, as he might have talked to Margery. And Muriel saw that she must be content with that for this night, and was happy and quiet beside him.

But when they parted under the wall it was she who whispered, 'Tomorrow – the last time,' and it was he who whispered, 'Yes.'

In the morning he woke with a vague sense of distaste for something that he had to do. All that day he had this restless, dissatisfied feeling. And this was in part the first stirring of the impulse to write which came always when he had no work in progress and no greater effort forming in his mind.

The weary reaction from the finishing of 'Chivalry' was over, and the creative itch was upon him, which could not be satisfied by the making of little Love-Songs. And he felt no more like the making of Love-Songs.

He wished almost that he might hurry immediately down to Hampshire. But his promise for the evening prevented that.

He sat down in the sunny window-seat

and thought, pondering gloomily the wild events of these summer months. And as he brooded over them with regret and sadness, and the beginnings of new resolutions, there flashed from them, with the electric suddenness of genuine inspiration, the bright spark of a new idea, a new idea for the new work which he was aching to begin. Thereon his mood of repentance faded away, and the moral aspect of the things he had done dissolved into the background – like fairies at a pantomime; and there was left the glowing vision of a work of art.

He was excited by this vision, and immediately was busy with a sheet of paper – like a painter capturing a first impression – jotting down in undecipherable half-words and initials the rough outline of his plan, even the names of his characters and a few odd phrases. There moved in his mind a seductive first line for the opening of this poem, and that line determined in the end the whole question of metre; for it was an inspired line, and it was in exactly the right metre.

All the afternoon he sat in the shady corner of the garden over the river, dreaming over the structure of this poem. In the evening he began to work upon it; and all the evening he worked, with a feverish concentration and excitement. At about ten o'clock the moon was well up, and the rising tide was lapping and murmuring already about the wall and about the boats. And he did not forget Muriel; he did not forget his promise. He knew that she was waiting for him, silent on the wall. He knew that he was bound in honour, or in dishonour, to go to her. But he did not go. He had done with that. And he had better things to do tonight.

So Muriel leaned lonely over the wall, looking down the river past the fig-tree and the barges, looking and listening. The moon rose high over Wimbledon, and the twin red lights of the *Stork* were lit, and the yellow lights twinkled in the houses and bobbed along the bridge, and the great tide rolled up with a rich suggestion of fulfilment and hope. Quiet couples drifted by in hired boats and were happy. But Stephen did not come. And Muriel waited.

St Peter's clock struck eleven, and still she waited, in a flame of longing and impatience. The dew came down, and she was cold; the chill of foreboding entered her heart. And still she waited. She would wait till half-past eleven, till a quarter to twelve, till midnight. She knew now that she loved this man with a deep and consuming love; it had begun lightly, as a kind of diversion, but the game had turned to bitter earnest. And still she waited.

It was slack water now, and the river stood still, holding its breath. Men passed singing along the towpath on the other side; the song floated over the water, in sentimental tones of exquisite melancholy. From the Island a wild duck rose with his mate, and bustled away with a startling whir to some sweet haunt among the reeds. A cat wailed at its wooing in a far garden – a sickly amorous sound. The last pair of lovers rowed slowly past, murmuring gently. Then all was still, and Muriel was left alone, alone of the world's lovers thwarted and forgotten.

Midnight struck, and she crept into the house and into her bed, sick with longing and the rage of shame.

Stephen at midnight went in contentment to his bed. He had written a hundred lines.

CHAPTER XIV

Lying in bed he made up his mind to go down to Margery the following Tuesday. But Margery, too, had been making up her mind. She wired at lunch time, and arrived herself at tea. She was tired, she said, of living alone in her Paradise. But she did not scold or question or worry him; so glad she was to be at home again with her Stephen. Stephen also was very glad, astonishingly glad, he felt. He greeted her and kissed her with a tender warmth which surprised them both. This sudden homecoming of his wife, of chattering Joan and bubbling Michael and comfortable old Nurse, and all that atmosphere of staid domesticity which they had brought with them into the house seemed to set an opportune seal on his new resolutions, on the final renunciation which he had made last night. It was the one thing wanted, he felt, to confirm him in virtue.

He took little Joan into the garden to see the rabbits. She was two and a half now, a bright and spirited child, with her mother's fairness and fragile grace, and something of Stephen's vitality. She greeted with delighted cries her old friends among the bunnies, Peter and Maud and Henry, and all their endless progeny, little grey bunnies and yellow bunnies and black bunnies, and tiny little brown bunnies that were mere scurrying balls of fur, coloured like a chestnut mare. The rabbit Peter and the rabbit Maud ran out of their corners and sniffed at her ankles, their noses twitching, as she stood in the sun. She stroked them and squeezed them and kissed them, and they bore it patiently in the expectation of food. But when they saw that she had no food, they stamped petulantly with their hind legs and ran off. Then she laughed her perfect inimitable laugh, and tried to coax the tiniest bunnies to come to her with a piece of decayed cabbage; and they pattered towards her in a doubtful crescent, their tiny noses twitching with the precise velocity of their parents' noses, their ears cocked forward in suspicion. When they had eddied back and forth for a little, like playful children defying the sea, they saw that the bait was indeed a rotten one, unworthy of the deed of daring which was asked of them, and they scuttled finally away into corners, where they lay heaving with their eyes slewed back, looking for danger. The rabbit Maud was annoyed by the clatter they made, and chased them impatiently about the run, nipping them viciously at the back of their necks; and the rabbit Peter, excited beyond bearing by the commotion, pursued the rabbit Maud as she pursued their young. Then they all stopped suddenly to nibble inconsequently at old bits of cabbage, or scratch their bellies, or scrabble vainly on the stone floor, or stamp with venom in the hutches, or lie full length and operate their noses. Little Joan loved them whatever they did, and Stephen, listening and watching while she gurgled and exclaimed, was sensible as he had never been before of the pride and privilege of being a father. The sight of his daughter playing with the young rabbits, young and playful and innocent as they, stirred him to an appropriate and almost mawkish remorse. For the great writer who, by his gifts of selection and restraint, can keep out from his writings all sentimentality and false emotion, cannot by the same powers keep them from his mind. Stephen Byrne, looking at innocence and thinking of his own wickedness, forgot his proportions, forgot the balanced realism which he put into everything he wrote, and swore to himself that by this sight he was converted, that by this revelation of innocence he, too, would be innocent again.

So they began again the quiet routine of domestic content, and Margery was very happy, putting out of her mind as an artist's madness the strange failure of Stephen to join her in the country. In the third week of September there were printed in the autumn number of a literary Quarterly 'Six Love-Songs,' by Stephen Byrne, which he had sent in hot haste to the editor on the morning of the Greenwich expedition. There was printed above them the dedication *'To M,'* and Margery as she read them was touched and melted with a great tenderness and pride. She would not speak of them to him, but she looked up, blushing, at the end of them and said only *'Stephen!'* And Stephen cursed himself in a hot shame for having thought them and written them and sent them to the paper. But since she liked them so well, and appreciated them as Muriel had never done, and since he persuaded himself that at this moment he might have written the same songs to his wife, so tenderly did he think of her now, he slowly came to forget the vicious squalor of their origin; and in time, when literary friends spoke of them and congratulated him (for they made a great stir) the shame had all gone, and he answered with a virtuous and modest pride, as if indeed they had been written to his wife – and so in fact he almost believed.

All September he worked steadily at the new poem. Very soon Margery asked if she might read as much as he had written. And at first he hesitated, and then he said that she might not.

Not till that moment did he realize the true character of what he was doing. The idea of the poem was very simple. He had taken the base history of his own life in this amazing summer, and was making of it a romantic and glorious poem. Everything was there – Emily and his cruelty to Emily, and the chivalry of John Egerton and his treachery to John, Margery, and Muriel, and his betrayal of both of them, and the second treachery to John in the stealing of Muriel. They were all there, and the deeds were there. But the names they bore were the names of old knights and fine ladies, moving generously through an age of chivalry and gallant ways; and the deeds he had done were invested with so rich a romance by the grace of and imagery and humanity of his verse, and by the gracious atmosphere of knighthood and adventure and forest battles which he wrapped about them, that they were beautiful. They were poetry. Himself in the story was a brave and legendary figure, Gelert by name, and Margery, the Princess, was his fair lady. And he had slain Emily by mischance in a forest encounter with another knight. He had hidden her body in a dark mysterious lake in the heart of the forest; this lake was beautifully described. John, his faithful companion was present and helped him, and because of the honour in which he held the Princess, he engaged to stay in the forest and do battle with the people of Emily if they should discover the crime, while Gelert rode off on some secret venture of an urgent and noble character. So John stayed, and was grievously wounded. But Gelert rode off to the castle of John's love and poisoned her mind against John, and wooed her and won her and flung her away when he was tired of her; but she loved him still too well to love any other from that day; and when John came to her she cast him out. More, because he was the companion-at-arms of Gelert, and she would do anything to wound Gelert, she sent word to the people of Emily that it was John indeed who had slain Emily, and they sought him out and slew him. But Gelert went home to his castle and swore great vows in passages of amazing dignity, and was absolved from his sins, and ruled the land for a long time in godly virtue, helping the weak and succouring the oppressed. And so finely was all this presented that at the end of it you felt but a conventional sympathy for the unfortunate John, while Gelert remained in the mind as a mixed, but on the whole a knightly character.

It was a lunatic excess of self-revelation, and Stephen was afraid of it. Nothing would have persuaded him to modify in any way his artistic purpose, and in his heart he flattered himself that the romantic disguise of his story was strong enough to protect it from the suggestion of reality. It would stand that test, he was sure. Yet he was not sure – not at any rate just now, with the sordid facts still fresh in his mind. Later, no doubt, when the thing was complete, and he could polish and prune it as a whole, he would be able to make himself absolutely safe. But just now, while the work was still shadowy and formless, he shrank from risking the revelations it might convey. To Margery most of all. Also, maybe, he was a little afraid that she would laugh at him.

And Margery said nothing, but wondered herself what it might mean.

John came home in the middle of September,

and called the same evening at the Tarrants' house. But he was told after a long wait that they were not at home.

The next morning, as he walked to the station, he passed in the street a parcel delivery van. On the front of it were the twin red posters of *I Say*, a weekly organ of the sensational patriotic type. It was a paper which did in fact a great deal of good in championing the cause of the underdog, yet at the same time impressing upon the underdog the highest constitutional principles. But it had to live. And it lived by the weekly promises of sensation which blazed at the public from the red posters all over England, and travelled everywhere on the front of delivery vans and the backs of buses. There was seldom more than a single sensation to each issue. But the very most was made of it by an ingenious contrivance of the editor, who himself arranged the wording of the posters; for each sensation he composed two and sometimes three quite different posters, cunningly devised so that any man who saw all three of them was as likely as not to buy the paper in the confident belief that he was getting for his penny three separate sensations.

The two posters that John saw ran as follows: one 'A CIVIL SERVANT'S NAME,' and the other 'OUR ROTTEN DETECTIVES.' At the station he saw another one specially issued to the West London paper stalls – 'MYSTERY OF HAMMERTON CHASE.' And at Charing Cross there was yet another – 'WHO OUGHT TO BE HANGED?'

John had no doubt of what he would find in the paper. He had wondered often at the long quiescence of the Gaunt family. Clearly they had taken their tale to the editor of *I Say*, and had probably been suitably compensated for their trouble and expense in bringing to the notice of the people's champion a shameful case of oppression and wrong.

So John walked on to the station with a strange feeling of lightness in the head and pain in his heart. At Hammersmith there was no copy of *I Say* to be had; at Charing Cross he bought two. The week's sensation was dealt with in a double-page article by the editor, diabolically clever. It set out at length the sparse facts of 'The Hammerton Mystery' as revealed at the inquest, with obsequious references to 'the genius of Stephen Byrne, the poet and prophet of Younger England'; and it contained some scathing comments on 'the crass ineptitude of our detective organization.' But it attacked no person, it imputed nothing. The sole concern of the editor was that 'months have passed and a hideous crime is yet unpunished. This poor girl went forth from her father and mother, and the young man who had promised to share her life; she went out into the world, innocent and fresh, to help her family in the battle of life with the few poor shillings she could earn by menial services in a strange house. It was not her fault that she was attractive to a certain type of man; but that attraction was no doubt her undoing. She took the fancy of some amorous profligate; she resisted his unknightly attentions; she was done to death. Her body was consigned in circumstances of the foulest indignity to a filthy grave in the river ooze.

'We are entitled to ask – What are the police doing? The matter has faded now from the public memory – has it faded from theirs? It is certain that it has not faded in the loyal hearts of the Gaunt family. At the time of the inquest the public were preoccupied with national events of the first importance, and the murder did not excite the attention it deserved. We have only too good reason to believe that our Criminal Investigation mandarins, supine as ever until they are goaded to activity by the spur of popular opinion, are taking advantage of that circumstance to allow this piece of blackguardly wickedness to sink for ever into oblivion. We do not intend that it should sink into oblivion, etc. etc.'

But in the tail of the article lay the personal

sting, cleverly concealed.

'But there is another aspect of this vile affair which we are compelled to notice. While the family of the murdered girl are nursing silently their broken hearts; while our inspectors and chief inspectors and criminal investigators are enjoying their comfortable salaries, there is a young man in Hammerton, a public servant of high character and irreproachable antecedents, over whom a black cloud of suspicion is hanging in connection with this crime. We cannot pretend that his evidence at the inquest was wholly satisfactory either in substance or in manner; it was shiftily given, and in the mind of any men less incompetent than the local coroner and the local dunderheads who composed the jury, would have raised questions of fundamental importance. But we are confident that John Egerton is innocent; and we say that it is a reproach to the whole system of British justice that he should still be an object of ignorant suspicion owing to the failure of the police-force to hound down the villain responsible for the crime.

'The fair name of a good citizen is at stake. It must be cleared.'

At the office there were whisperings and curious looks; and John's chiefs conferred in dismay on a position of delicacy that was unexampled in their official experience.

John went home early, with his *I Say*'s crumpled in his pocket. And there he found the Rev. Peter Tarrant striding about impatiently with a copy open on the table before him. His head moved about like a great bat just under the low roof, his jolly red face was as full of anger as it could ever be.

'Look here, John,' he roared, 'what are you going to do about this – this MUCK?'

'Nothing.'

In truth he had thought little of what he was going to do; he had been too angry and bewildered and ashamed. Only he had sworn vaguely to himself that whatever happened he would stand by his old determination to keep this business from Margery. And, now that the question was put to him, the best way of doing that was clearly to do nothing. He began to think of reasons for doing nothing.

The Rev. Peter thundered again, *'Nothing?* But you *must* – you must do – something.' He stuttered with impotent rage and brought his fist down on *I Say* with a titanic force, so that the table jumped and the Wedgwood plate clattered on the dresser. 'You can't sit down under this sort of thing – you must bring an action–'

'Can't afford it; it would cost me a thousand if I won – and five thousand if – if I lost.'

'If you *lost!*' The Rev. Peter looked at him in wonder. John tried to look him straight in the face, but his glance wavered in the shy distress of an innocent man who suspects the beginnings of doubt in a friend's mind.

'Yes – you know what a Law Court is – anything may happen – and I should never make a good show in the witness box, if I stood there for ever.'

'I don't care – you can't sit down under it. You'll lose your job, won't you – for one thing?'

'No – I don't know – I can't help it if I do.'

'Well, if you don't lose that you'll lose Muriel.' The Rev. Peter lowered his voice. 'Look here, I want you two to fix things up. I've just been to see her – she looks unhappy – she's lonely, I believe, with that damned old mother of hers. But you can't expect her to marry you with this sort of thing going about uncontradicted.'

And at that John wavered. But he thought of Margery and his knightly vow, and he thought of the witness box; of himself stammering and shifting hour after hour in that box; of pictures in the Press; of columns in the Press; of day after day of public wretchedness – the inquest over again infinitely enlarged. And the thought of the open, perhaps inevitable, ignominy of losing a libel action. And he was sure that he was right.

They argued about this for a long time, and the Rev. Peter yielded at last.

But he bellowed then, 'Well, you must write them a letter at once. Sit down now, and I'll dictate it. Sit down, will you? By God, it makes me sweat, this!'

John sat down meekly and wrote to the editor of *I Say*, as the Rev. Peter commanded. The Rev. Peter dictated in the round tones of a man practising a speech:

'DEAR SIR, – I have seen your infamous article. It is a cruel and disgusting libel. I wish to state publicly that I had nothing to do with the death of Emily Gaunt; that so far as I know no suspicion does rest upon me here or elsewhere; and that, if indeed there is suspicion, it is not in the minds of anyone whose opinion I value, and I can therefore ignore it. In any case I should prefer to do without your dirty assistance.'

'Can't say "dirty" – can we?' said John.

'Why not? They *are* dirt – filth – muck! Well, then – put "dishonouring" – "your dishonouring assistance." Go on:

'I am not a rich man, and I cannot afford to bring an action for libel against you. A successful suit would cost me far more money and trouble than I should like to waste upon it. You, on the other hand, could easily afford to lose and would probably be actually benefited by a substantial increase in your circulation.

'I must ask you to print this letter in your next issue and insist also on an unqualified apology for your use of my name.

'I am sending this letter to the local Press.'

The editor of *I Say* did not print this letter, as the Rev. Peter had fondly imagined he would, but he referred in his second article, which was similar to the first, only more outspoken, to 'the receipt of an abusive letter from the suspected person.'

Slowly that week a copy of *I Say* found its way into every house in The Chase; and the article was read and discussed and argued about, and the whole controversy of May, which had been almost forgotten, sprang into life again. And the following week the local papers were bought and borrowed and devoured, and John's spirited and courageous letter was admired and laughed at and condemned. The Chase fell again into factions, though now the Whittaker (pro-John) faction was the stronger. For nobody liked *I Say*, though it was always exciting to read when there was some special excuse for bringing it into the house. Besides, the honour of The Chase was now at stake.

John and the Rev. Peter had reckoned without the generosity and communal feeling of the people of The Chase. They were never so happy as when they had some communal enterprise on foot, a communal kitchener, or a communal crèche or a communal lawsuit, some joint original venture which offered reasonable opportunities for friendly argument and committee meetings and small subscriptions. This spirit had of course unlimited scope during the war, and perhaps it was the communal Emergency Food-Kitchen that had been its most ambitious and perfect expression. But it lived on vigorously after the war. Several of the busiest and earliest workers among the men shared a communal taxi into town every day. There was a communal governess, and one or two semi-communal boats. There was also a kind of communal Housing Council, which met whenever a house in The Chase was to be let or sold, and exerted pressure on the outgoing tenant as to his choice of a successor. Outside friends of The Chase who desired and were desired to come into residence were placed upon a roster by the Housing Council, and when the Council's edict had once gone forth, the outgoing tenant was expected at all costs to see that the chosen person was enabled to succeed him, and if he did not, or if he allowed the owner of the house to enter into some secret arrangement with an outsider, unknown and unapproved by the Council, it was a sin against the solidarity of The Chase.

And there had already been a communal lawsuit, that great case of *Stimpson and Others* versus *The Quick Boat Company* –an action for nuisance brought by the entire Chase, because of the endless and intolerable noise and smell of the defendant company's motor-boats, which they manufactured half a mile up the river and exercised all day snorting and phutting and dashing about with loud and startling reports in the narrow reach between the Island and The Chase.

Nine gallant champions had stood forward with Stimpson for freedom and The Chase. But all The Chase had attended the preliminary meetings; all The Chase had subscribed; all The Chase and all their wives had given evidence in Court; and before this unbroken, or almost unbroken, front (for there were a few black sheep) the Quick Boat Company had gone down heavily. Judgment for the plaintiffs had been given in the early spring.

So that when it was widely understood that for lack of money John Egerton, a member of The Chase, was unable to defend himself from a scurrilous libel in a vulgar paper, the deepest instincts of the neighbourhood were aroused. A small informal Committee met at once at the Whittakers' house – Whittaker and Mr Dimple (for legal advice) and

Andrews and Tatham and Henry Stimpson. Stephen Byrne was asked to come, but had an engagement.

Mr Dimple's advice was simple. He said that subject to certain reservations – as to which he would not bother the Committee, since they related rather to the incalculable niceties of the law, and lawyers, as they knew, were always on the nice side (laughter – but not much) – and assuming that Mr Egerton won his case, as to which he would express no opinion, though as a man he might venture to say that he knew of no one in The Chase – he had almost said no one in London – of whom it would be more unfair – he would not put it stronger than that, for he liked to assume that even a paper such as *I Say* was sincere and honest at heart – to make the kind of suggestion which he knew and they all knew had been made in that paper, about Mr Egerton – a quiet, God-fearing, honest citizen – but they all knew him as well as he did, so he would say no more about that – subject then to what he had said first and assuming what he had just said – and bearing in mind the proverbial – he thought he might say proverbial (Dickens, after all, was almost a proverb) uncertainties and surprises of his own profession, he thought they would not be wildly optimistic or unduly despondent – and for himself he wanted to be neither – if they estimated the costs of the action at a thousand pounds, but of course–

Waking up at the word 'pounds' – the kind of word for which they had been subconsciously waiting – the Committee began the process of unravelling which was always necessary after one of Mr Dimple's discourses. And their conclusion was that it was up to The Chase to subscribe as much of the money as possible, as much at any rate as would enable John Egerton to issue a writ without the risk of financial ruin.

Henry Stimpson was naturally deputed to collect the money. Stimpson was an indefatigable man, a laborious Civil Servant who worked from 10 till 7.30 every day (and took his lunch at the office), yet was not only ready but pleased to spend his evenings and his weekends, canvassing for subscriptions, writing whips for meetings, or working out elaborate calculation of the amount due to Mrs Ambrose in money and kind on her resigning from the communal kitchen after paying the full subscription and depositing a ham in the Committee's charge which had been cooked by mistake and sent to Mrs Vincent. He genuinely enjoyed this kind of task, and he did it very, very well.

Henry Stimpson duly waited on the Byrnes and explained the position. Stephen Byrne had read the articles in *I Say*, and

Margery had read them. And a gloom had fallen upon Stephen, for which Margery was unable wholly to account as a symptom of solicitude for his friend's troubles – especially as they never seemed to see each other nowadays. To her knowledge they had not met at all since the summer holidays.

Nor had they. They avoided each other. This resurrection of the Emily affair, these articles and the new publicity, and now on top of that the prospect of a libel action, was to Stephen like a slap in the face. He had almost forgotten his old anxieties in the absorption of work and the soothing atmosphere of his new resolutions. But he would not go to John; he had been lucky before; he might be lucky again; he would wait. Old John might be trusted to do nothing precipitate.

So he promised to subscribe to the fund for the defence of John Egerton's good name, and Stimpson went away. The money was to be collected by that day week, and on the following Thursday there would be a general meeting to consider a plan of campaign. Stimpson's eyes as he spoke of 'a general meeting' were full of quiet joy.

And Stephen went on with his work – very slowly now, but he went on. The poem was nearly finished; he had only to polish it a little. But he sat now for long minutes glowering and frowning over his paper, staring out of the window, staring at nothing. Margery, watching him, wondered yet more what work he was at, and what was the secret of this gloom. She began to think that the two things might be connected; he might be attempting some impossible task; he might be overworked and stale. This had happened before. But in his worst hours of artistic depression he had never looked so black as sometimes she saw him now. And she noticed that he tried to conceal this mood from her; he would manufacture a smile if he caught her watching him. And that, too, was unusual.

Then one evening when she went to her table for some small thing she saw there the unmistakable manuscript of this new work lying in an irregular heap on the blotter. Her eyes were caught by the title – 'The Death in the Wood' – written in large capitals at the head; and almost without thinking she read the first line. And she read the few following lines. Then, urged on by an uncontrollable curiosity and excitement, she read on. She sat down at the table and read, threading a slow way through a maze of alterations and erasions, and jumbles of words enclosed in circles on the margin or at the bottom or at the top and wafted with arrows and squiggly lines into their intended positions. But she understood the strange language of creative manuscript, and she read through the whole of the first section – Gelert riding through the forest, the battle in the forest, and the death of the maiden. And as she read she was deeply moved. She forgot the problem of Stephen's gloom in her admiration and affectionate pride.

At the end of it Gelert stood sorrowing over the body and made a speech of intense dignity and poetic feeling. And at that point she heard the voice of Stephen at the front door, and started away, remembering suddenly that this reading was a breach of confidence. But why – why was she not allowed to see it?

Yet that, after all, was a small thing; and she went to bed very happy, dreaming such golden dreams of the success of the poem as she might have dreamed if she had written it herself.

CHAPTER XV

The Chase was true to its highest traditions. Before the week was over it was known that the sum determined on by the Egerton Defence Fund Committee had been already promised, and more.

Stephen Byrne, with a heavy heart, went to the 'general meeting' on Tuesday evening.

To have stayed away would have looked odd; also he was anxious to know the worst. He walked there as most men go to a battle, full of secret foreboding, yet dubiously glad of the near necessity for action. If, indeed, there was to be a libel action, backed by all the meddlesome resources of The Chase, things would have to come to a head. This was a development which had never been provided for in his calculation and plans. It would have been easier, somehow, if John had been arrested, charged by the Crown with murder. He would have known then what to do – or he thought he would. He wished now that he had been to see John, found out what he was thinking. But he was nervous of John now, or rather he was nervous of himself. He could not trust himself not to do something silly if he met John in private again; the only thing to do was to try to forget him, laugh at him if possible. And that was the devil of this libel business. He would have to be there himself, he would have to give evidence again, and sit there probably while poor old John was stammering and mumbling in the box. Yet he had done it before – why not again? Somehow he felt that he could not do it again. It all seemed different now.

And that poem! Why the hell had he written it? Why had he sent it to *The Argus*. He had had it typed on Thursday, and sent it off by special messenger on Friday, just in time for the October number. *The Argus* liked long poems. What a fool he had been! Or had he? He knew very well himself what it all meant – but how could anyone else connect it with life – with Emily Gaunt? No, that was all right. And it was damned good stuff! He was glad he had sent it. It would go down well. And another day would have meant missing the October number.

Yes, it was damned good stuff! He stood at the Whittakers' door, turning over in his head some favourite lines from Gelert's speech in the forest. Damned good! As he thought how excellent it was, there was a curious sensation of tingling and contraction in the flesh of his body and the back of his legs.

When he came out, an hour later, he was a happier man. He was almost happy. For it had been announced at the meeting, with all the solemnity of shocked amazement that Mr Egerton had refused to avail himself of the generous undertaking of The Chase and neighbourhood. The money promised would enable him to sue with an easy mind. But he would not sue.

There was nothing to be done, then, but put and carry votes of thanks to the un-official Committee for their labour and enterprise, to Whittaker for the use of his house, to Henry Stimpson for his wasted efforts. The last of these votes was felt by most to be effort equally wasted, since they knew well that Henry Stimpson had in fact thoroughly enjoyed collecting promises and cash, and had now the further unlooked-for delight of having to return the money already subscribed.

This done, the meeting broke up with a sense that they had been thwarted, or at any rate unreasonably debarred from a legitimate exercise of their communal instincts.

But apart from this intelligible disappointment there was a good deal of head-shaking, and plain, if not outspoken, disapproval of Egerton's conduct. Stephen, moving among the crowd, gathered easily the sense of The Chase, and it had veered surprisingly since Whittaker's announcement. For John Egerton had advanced, it seemed, the astounding reason that he might *lose* the case. To the simple people of The Chase – as indeed to the simple population of England – there was only one test to a libel action. Either you won or you lost. The complex cross-possibilities of justification and privilege and fair comment and the rest of it, which Mr Dimple was heard to be apologetically explaining in a corner to a deaf lady, were lost upon them. If you failed to win your case, what the other man said was true, and if you were not confident of winning, your conscience could not be absolutely clear. The meeting rather felt that John Egerton had let them down, but they were certain that he had let himself down. And it was clear that even his staunchest supporters, men like Whittaker and Tatham, were shaken in their allegiance.

But Stephen Byrne was happy. He had trusted to luck again, and luck, or rather the quixotic lunacy of John Egerton, had saved him again. It was wonderful. It was all over now. John had finally made his bed, and he must lie on it. He thought little of what this must mean to John, this aggravation of the local suspicions. He saw only one thing, that yet another wall had been raised between himself and exposure, that once more his anxieties might be thrust into the background. That he might settle down again with a comfortable mind to literature and domestic calm. He had forgotten with his fears his compunction of an hour ago; he had forgotten even to feel grateful to John; and if he thought of him with pity, it was a contemptuous pity. He saw John now as a kind of literary figure of high but laughable virtue, a man so virtuous as to be ridiculous, a mere foil to the heroic dare-devils of life – such as Gelert and Stephen Byrne.

So he came to his own house, thinking again of those excellent lines of Gelert's speech. In the hall he composed in his mind the description of the meeting which he would give to Margery.

But Margery, too, was thinking of Gelert. She was reading the manuscript of 'The Death in the Wood.' She had watched Stephen go out in a slow gloom to the meeting, and then she had hurried to the table and taken guiltily the bundle from the special manuscript drawer. For Stephen, with the sentimental fondness of many writers for the original work of their own hands, preserved his manuscripts long after they had been copied in type and printed and published. Twice during the last week she had gone to that drawer, but each time she had been interrupted. And at each reading her curiosity and admiration had grown.

She had suspected nothing – had imagined no sort of relation between Stephen's life and Gelert's adventures. There was no reason why she should. For she detested – as she had been taught by Stephen to detest – the conception of art as a vast auto-biography. Stephen's personality was in the feeling and in the phrasing of his work; and that was enough for her; the substance was a small matter.

–Even the incident of the maiden in the wood, her death and her concealment in the lake, had scarcely stirred the memory of Emily. For the reverent and idyllic scene in which the two knights had 'laid' the body of the maiden among the reeds and water lilies of the lake, to be discovered by her kinsmen peeping through the tangled thickets of wild rose, was as remote as possible from the sordid ugliness of Emily's disposal and discovery in a muddy sack near Barnes.

But now she had finished. And she did suspect. When she came to the passage describing Gelert's remorse for the betrayal of his old companion-at-arms, his gloomy bearing and penitent vows, she thought suddenly of Stephen's late extravagant gloom, which she was still unable to understand. And then she suspected. Idly the thought came, and idly she put it away. But it returned, and she hated herself because of it. It grew to a stark suspicion, and she sat for a moment in an icy terror, frozen with pain by her imaginations. Then in a fever of anxiety she went back to the beginning of the manuscript, and hurried through it again, noting every incident of the story in the hideous light of her suspicions. And as she turned over the untidy pages, the terror grew.

In the light of this dreadful theory so many things were explained – little odd things which had puzzled her and been forgotten – Stephen's surprising anxiety when Michael was born (and Emily disappeared), and that evening in the summer, when they had all been so silent and awkward together, and the

243

drifting apart of Stephen and John, and John's extraordinary evidence, and Stephen's present depression. It was all so terribly clear, and the incidents of the poem so terribly fitted in. Margery moaned helplessly to herself, 'Oh, *Stephen!*' When he came in, she was almost sure.

It was curious that at first she thought nothing of Gelert's illicit amours in the castle, the stealing of his own friend's lady. That part of the poem, of course, was a piece of romantic imagination, with which she had no personal concern. But while she waited for Stephen, turning over the leaves one more, the thought did come to her, 'If one part is true – why not all?' But this thought she firmly thrust out. She was sure of him in *that* way, at any rate. She flung a cushion over the manuscript and waited.

He came in slowly as he had gone out, but she saw at once that his gloom was somehow relieved. And as he told her in studied accents of distress the story of the meeting, there came to her a sick certainty that he was acting. He was not *really* sorry that John had thought it best not to take any action; he was glad.

When he had finished, she said, in a hard voice which startled her, 'What *do* you make of it, Stephen? Do you think he really did it?'

Stephen looked at the fire, the first fire of

late September, and he said, 'God knows, Margery; God knows. He's a funny fellow, John.' He sighed heavily and stared into the fire.

And then she was quite sure.

She stood up from the sofa, the manuscript in her hand, and came towards him.

'Stephen,' she said, 'I've been reading this–You – I – oh, *Stephen!*'

The last word come with a little wail, and she burst suddenly into tears, hiding her face against his shoulder. She stood there sobbing, and shaken with sobbing, and he tried to soothe her, stroking her hair with a futile caressing movement, and murmuring her name ridiculously, over and over again.

It did not occur to him to go on acting, to pretend astonishment or incomprehension. She had blundered somehow on the secret, and perhaps it was better so. To her at least he could lie no more.

At last the sobbing ceased, and he kissed her gently, and she turned from him automatically to tidy her hair in the glass.

Then she said, still breathless and incoherent, 'Stephen, is it true – that poor Emily – and poor John– Oh, Stephen, how *could* you?'

The tears were coming back, so he put his arms about her again. And he spoke quickly, anything to hold her attention and keep away those terrible tears.

'Darling, I was a fool ... it was for your sake in the first place – for your sake we kept it dark, I mean – it was John's idea – and then– I don't know– I was a beast– But don't worry. Tomorrow I'll put it all right... I'll give myself up – I–'

But at these words, and at the picture they raised, a great cry burst from her, 'Oh no, Stephen. No! no! – you mustn't.'

And she seized the lapels of his coat and shook him fiercely in the intensity of her feeling, the human, passionate, protective feeling of a wife for her own man – careless what evil he may have done if somehow he may be made safe for her.

And Stephen was startled. He had not expected this. He said, stupidly, 'But John – what about John? – don't you want me – don't you–?'

'No, Stephen, no – at least–' and she stopped, thinking now of John, trying conscientiously to realize what was owed to him. Then she went on, in a broken torrent of pleading, 'No, Stephen, it's gone on so long now – a little more won't matter to him – surely, Stephen – and nobody *really* thinks he did it – *nobody*, Stephen. It's only people like Mrs Vincent, Mrs Ambrose was saying so only yesterday – and it would mean – it would mean – what *would* it mean, Stephen – Stephen, tell me?' But as she imagined what this would mean to Stephen she stood shuddering before him, her big eyes staring piteously at him.

'It would mean – O God, Margery, I don't kno –' and he turned away.

So for a long time she pleaded with him, in groping, inarticulate half-sentences. She never reproached him, never asked him how he had come to do a foul murder. She did not want to know that, she did not want to think of what it was *right* for him to do – that was too dangerous. All that mattered was this danger – a danger that could be avoided if she could only persuade him. And Stephen listened in a kind of stupor, listened miserably to the old excuses and arguments, and half-truths with which he had so often in secret convinced himself. But somehow, as Margery put them with all the prejudice of her passionate fears, they did not convince him. They stood out horribly in their nakedness. And though he was touched and amazed by the strength of her forgiveness and her love in the face of this knowledge, he wished almost that she had not forgiven him, had urged him with curses to go out and do his duty. No, he did not wish that, really. But he did wish she would leave him alone now, leave him to think. He *must* think.

His eye fell on the manuscript lying on the floor, and he began to wonder what it was in the poem that had told her, and how much it had told. She had said nothing of that. He interrupted her: 'How – how did you guess?' He jerked his head at the paper.

She told him. And as she went again through that terrible process in her mind, that other thought returned, that idle notion about the wooing in the castle, which she had flung away from her.

She said, faltering and slow, her lips trembling, 'Stephen –there's nothing else in it ... is there? ... I ought to have guessed? – Stephen, you *do* love me don't you?' She stepped uncertainly towards him, and then with a loud cry, 'Darling, I *do!*' he caught her to him. And she knew that it was true.

CHAPTER XVI

In the morning he went out as usual to feed the sea-gulls before breakfast, as if nothing had happened or was likely to happen. He was pleased as usual to see from the window that they were waiting for him, patient dots of grey and white, drifting on the near water. The sun broke thinly through the October haze, and the birds circled in a chattering crowd against the gold. And he had as usual the sense of personal satisfaction when they caught in the air, with marvellous judgment and grace, the pieces of old bread he flung out over the water, and was disappointed as usual when they missed it, and the bread fell into the river, though even then it was delightful to see with how much delicacy they skimmed over, and plucked it from the surface as they flew, as if it were a point of honour not to settle or pause or wet their red feet, tucked back beneath them.

And he had breakfast as usual with Margery and chattering Joan, and as usual afterwards went out with Joan to feed the rabbits, and again enjoyed the mysterious and universal pleasure of giving food to animals and watching them eat. He noted as usual the peculiar habits and foibles of the rabbit Henry and the rabbit Maud, and the common follies of all of them – how they all persisted, as usual, in crowding impossibly round the same cabbage leaf, jostling and thrusting and eating with the maximum discomfort, with urgent anxiety and petulant stamping because there were too many of them, while all around there lay large wet cabbage leaves, inviting and neglected. He listened as usual to little Joan's insane interminable questions, and answered them as usual as intelligently as he could. And he puffed as usual at the perfect pipe of after-breakfast, and swept as usual the dead leaves from the path. But all these things he did with the exquisite melancholy enjoyment of a schoolboy, knowing that he does them for the last time on the last day of his holidays at home.

And he had decided nothing. Margery, too, moved as usual through the busy routine of after-breakfast, 'ordering' food for herself and Stephen and the children and the servants, and promising Cook to get some lard, and 'speaking to' Mary about the drawing-room carpet, and arranging for the dining-room to be 'done out' tomorrow, and conferring with Nurse, and telephoning for some fish. She did these things in a kind of dream, hating them more than usual, and now and then she looked out of the window, and wondered what Stephen was doing, and what he was thinking. For she knew that he had not decided. And she would not speak to him; she had said her say, and some instinct told her that silence now was her best hope.

So all day they went about in this distressful tranquillity, pretending that this day was as yesterday, and as the day before. At midday the tide was down; the grey sky crept up from the far roofs and hid the sun. There was the damp promise of a drizzle in the air, and the bleak depression of low tide lay over the mud and meagre stream and the deserted boats. They had lunch almost in silence, and after lunch a thin rain began.

Stephen stared out at it silent from the window, thinking and thinking and deciding nothing; and Margery sat silent by the fire, darning. And her silence, and the silent riot of his thoughts, and the silent miserable rain, and the empty abandoned river, united in a vast conspiracy of menace and accusation and gloom. They were leagued together to get on his nerves and drive him to despair. He went out suddenly, and down to the dining-room, and there he drank some whisky, very quickly, and very strong.

Then, because he must do *something* or he would go mad, he dragged the dinghy over the mud and shingle down to the water, and rowed up to the Island to pick up firewood from the mud-banks, where the high tides took it and left it tangled in the reeds and young willow stems.

It was an infinite toil to get this wood, but all afternoon he worked there, crashing fiercely through the tall forest of withies and crowded reeds, and slithering down banks into deep mud, and groping laboriously in the slush of small inlets for tiny pieces of tarred wood, and filling his basket with great beams and bits of bark, and small planks and box-wood, and painfully carrying them through the mud and the wet reeds down to the boat. He worked hard, with a savage determination to tire himself, to occupy his mind, cursing with a kind of furious satisfaction when the stems sprang back and whipped him in the face. The sweat came out upon him, and his hands were scratched, and the mud was thick upon his clothes. But all the time he thought. He could not stop thinking.

And somehow the fierce energy of the work communicated itself to his thoughts. As he struck down the brittle reeds he fancied himself striking at his enemies, manfully meeting his Fate. All his life he had done things thoroughly, as he was doing this foolish wood-gathering. He had faced things, he had not been afraid. He would not be afraid now. He would give himself up. No, no! He couldn't do that. Not fair to Margery – a long wait, prison, trial, the dock – hanging! Aah! He made a shuddering cry at that thought, and he lashed out with the stick in his hand, beating at the withies in a fury of fear. No, no! by God, no! – hanging – the last morning! Not that.

But still, he must be brave. No more cowardice. That was the worst of all he had done this summer – the cowardice. No more sitting tight at John's expense. Whatever Margery said. It was sweet of her, but later it would be different. When all this was forgotten, she would remember ... she would be living with him, day after day, knowing every night there was a murderer in her bed, a liar, a coward, a treacherous coward... Very soon she would hate him. And he would hate her, because she knew. He would be always ashamed before her, all day, always... Just now they did not mind, because they were afraid. But they *would* mind... She had not even minded about Muriel, when he told her – and he had told her everything. But she would mind that, too, in the end... She would always be imagining Muriels.

No, there must be no more cowardice. It must finish now, one way or another. But there was only one way.

The rain had stopped now, and a warm wind blew freshly from the south-west. The two swans of the Island washed themselves in the ruffled shallows, wings flapping and necks busily twisting. In the west was a stormy and marvellous sky, still dark pillows of heavy clouds, black and grey, and an angry purple, with small white tufts floating irresponsibly across them, and here and there a startling lake of the palest blue; while low down, beneath them, as if rebellious at the long grey day, and determined somehow to make a show at his own setting, the sun revealed himself as an orange dome on the roof of the Quick Boat Company, and, poised grotesquely between the tall black chimneys, flung out behind the Richmond Hills a narrow ribbon of defiant light, and away towards Hammersmith all the windows in a big house lit up suddenly with orange and gold, as if the house were burning furiously within. The boat was heavy now with wood, and Stephen pushed her off to row home with his face to the sunset and the storm. Now the light was caught in the mud-slopes by the Island, and they, too, were beautiful. And as he rowed he said a self-conscious farewell to the sun and the warm wind and the river which he loved. No one loved this river as he did. They lived snugly in their drawing-rooms like Kensington people, and they looked out at the river when the sun shone at high tide, and in the summer crept out timidly for an hour in hired boats like trippers. But when it was winter and the wind blew, they drew their curtains and shivered over their fires and shut out the river, so that they hardly knew it was there from the autumn to the spring. They did not deserve to live by the river; they did not understand it. They did not see that it was lovable always, and most lovable perhaps when the tide rushed in against the wild west wind, and the rain and the spindrift lashed your face as you tossed in a small boat over the lively waves. They thought it was the noisy storm rushing down a muddy river; they thought the wind made a melancholy howl about the windows. They did not know that the river in the wind was a place of poetry and excitement, such as you might not find in the rest of London, that the noisy wind and the muddy water and the wet mud at low tide were things of beauty and healthy life if you went out and made friends with them. These people never saw the sunset in winter, and the curious majesty of factories against the glow; they never saw the lights upon the mud; they did not love the barges and the tugs, sliding up with a squat importance out of the fog, or swishing lazily down in the early morning, with the hoarfrost thick upon their decks. They did not know what the river was like in the darkness or the winter dusk; you could not know that till you had been on the river many times at those hours and found out the strange lights and the strange whispers, and the friendly loneliness of the river in the dark.

And when he had gone, no one here would do that; no one would row out in the frosty noons or the velvet dusks, no one would feed the sea-gulls in the morning, or steal out in the evening to watch the dab-chicks diving round the Island. No one would be left who properly loved the river. They would sit in their drawing-rooms and shudder at the wind, and say: 'That poor fellow Byrne – he was mad about the river – he was always pottering about on the river in a boat – and then, you know, he drowned himself in the river – just outside here.' Yes, he would do that. There would be something 'dramatic' about that. Just outside here – in the dark. He had decided now. Not poison, for he knew nothing about that; not shooting – for he had no revolver. But the river.

When he had decided his heart was lighter. Very carefully he moored the boat, and took out the wood and carried it in a basket to the kitchen to be dried. Then he took a last look at the river and the sun and went into tea. All that evening he was very cheerful with Margery in the drawing-room, and at dinner and afterwards. At dinner he talked hard and laughed very often. And Margery was easier in her mind, though sometimes she was puzzled by his laughter. But she thought that she had persuaded him, or that he had persuaded himself, that she was right, and this gaiety was the reaction from the long uncertainty of mind. And indeed it was. She saw also that he drank a good deal; but because he was cheerful at last, and would be more cheerful when he had drunk more, she did not mind.

By the late post there came a copy of *The Argus*. They looked at the parcel, but they did not open it, and they did not look at each other.

When she went up to bed he kissed her fondly, but not too fondly, lest she should suspect – and said that he would sit and read for a little by the fire. Then he opened *The Argus* and read through 'The Death in the Wood' from beginning to end. It pleased him now – it pleased him very much; for it was more than a week since he had seen it, and some of its original freshness had returned. It was good. But it seemed to him, as he read it now, to be a very damning confession of weakness and sin. And while he glowed with the pride of artistic achievement, he was chilled with the shame of his human record. It was so clear and naked in this poem that he had written; it was obvious to any who read it what kind of a man he was and what things he had done. Margery had known, and surely the whole world would know. But no matter – he would be too quick for them. He would be dead before they discovered.

And anyhow he was going to tell the world. Of course, he had forgotten that. He was going to tell the truth about John before he went. Of course. He must do that now.

He took some writing-paper and went down into the dining-room. He felt a little cold – not so cheerful. A little whisky would buck him up. A little whisky, while he wrote this letter.

He drank half a tumbler, and sat down. How would it go, this letter? To the police, of course. He wrote:

'This is to certify that I, Stephen Byrne,

strangled Emily Gaunt on the 15th May; John Egerton had nothing to do with it. I am going to drown myself.'

He signed it and read it over. After 'strangled' he squeezed in 'by accident.' It looked untidy, and he wrote it all out again. That would do. He drank some more whisky and sat staring at the paper.

Why should he do that? Wasn't he going to do enough, as it was? He was going to die; that was surely punishment enough. Why should he leave this damned silly confession behind? Just for the sake of old John. Damn John! A good fellow, John. A damned fool, John. Was it fair to Margery? That was the thing. Was it fair? One more drink.

He filled up the fourth glass and sat pondering stupidly the supreme selfishness. Outside the wind had risen, and Margery shivered upstairs at the rattle of the windows. Eleven o'clock – why was Stephen so long? What was that noise? A dull report – like a distant bomb. She sat up in bed, listening. Then she remembered. The gas-stove being lit in the dining-room. Something was wrong with it. But why had it frightened her? And why was it being lit?

Because it was cold in the dining-room, and the wind was howling, and there was a numb sensation in his hands. A funny, dead feeling. The whisky, perhaps. But when he had turned on the gas, he forgot about it, and stood thinking, match-box in hand, thinking out the new problem. It was difficult to think clearly. Then it exploded like that, when he put the match to it. He kicked it. Damned fool of a thing. Like John. It was John who was responsible for all this worry and fuss. John could go to the devil. He had fooled John before, and he would fool him again. Ha, ha! That was a cunning idea. Then they would say in the papers, 'A great genius – a noble character – ha, ha! – 'The Death in the Wood' – last work, imaginative writing' – ha, ha! *imaginative!* – and it was all true. But nobody would know – nobody would say so – because he would be dead. John wouldn't say so, and Margery wouldn't say so – because he would be dead. Mustn't say anything about the dead. Oh no! Must burn this silly confession. When he had had another drink. It was so cold. No more whisky – hell! 'There's hoosh in the bottle still.' But there wasn't. Who wrote that? Damned Canadian fellow. The Yukon. Port. There was some port somewhere. Port was warming.

He fumbled in the oak dresser for the decanter, knocking over a number of glasses. Damned little port left – somebody been at it. Best drink in the world – port. Good, rich, generous stuff. Ah! That was good. One more glass. Then he would go out. Half-past eleven. Margery would be wandering down in a minute – would think he was drunk. He wasn't drunk – head perfectly clear. Saw the whole thing now. Dramatic end – drowned in sight of home – national loss – moonlight. No, there was no moon. Hell of a wind, though. A sou'wester – he, he! Poor Margery, poor Muriel, poor John! They would miss him – when he had gone. They would be sorry then. Good fellow, John. Good fellows – all of them; But they didn't appreciate him – nobody did. Yes, Muriel did. A dear girl, Muriel. But no mind. He would like to say good-bye to Muriel. And Margery. But that wouldn't do. Dear things, both of them. Drink their healths. The last glass. No more port. No more whisky. No cheese, no butter, no jam. Like the war. Ha, ha!

First-rate port. He was warm now, and sleepy. God, what a wind. Mustn't go to sleep here. Sleep in the river – the dear old river. Drowning was pleasant, they said – not like hanging. Would rather stay here, though – in the warm. Only there was no more port. And he had promised some one – *must* keep promises. Come on, then. No shirking. Head perfectly clear. What was it he was going to do first? Something he had to do. God knows. Head perfectly clear. But sleepy. Terribly sleepy.

He walked over with an intense effort of steadiness to the door into the garden, as if there were many watching, and opened the door. The wind beat suddenly in his face and rushed past triumphant into the house. The bay-tree tossed and shook itself in the next garden. The dead leaves rushed rustling up and down the stone path, and leapt in coveys up the wall, and fled for refuge up the steps and into the house out of the furious wind. The shock of the cool air and the violence of the wind sobered him a little, and he paused irresolutely at the top of the steps. Then, with the obstinate fidelity of a drunken man to a purpose once formed, he walked unsteadily down the steps; he looked up at the lighted window of Margery's room, and waved his arm vaguely, and shouted a thick 'Good-bye,' but his throat was husky, and it was difficult to shout. Then he passed on down the path, talking to himself There was a boathook against the wall and he picked it up, and went down the steps into the small dinghy. He fumbled for a long time with the rope that tied her, and pushed off at last with the boathook. He pushed out into the wind, stupidly paddling with the boathook, because he had forgotten the oars. But it was no matter. He would not go back. He must go on. Out into the middle.

Margery, lying wondering in bed, heard the faint sound of a cry above the wind, and jumped out of bed. From the window she saw nothing but the hurrying clouds and the faint, wild gleam of the excited river. She crept down shivering to the drawing-room, where the lights still burned. A great draught of cold air swept up to the stairs, and she ran down fearfully to the dining-room. She saw the glasses in the brilliant light, the empty glasses and the empty bottle and the empty decanter, and under one of the glasses a sheet of paper flapping in the wind. She picked it up, stained with a wet half-circle of wine, and then with a low wail she ran out through the open door into the roaring gloom, her thin covering whipping about her.

It was dark in the garden, but over the river there was the pale radiance of water in the wind. And there were some stars now, racing after the clouds. And away towards the Island she saw the boat, not far off, a small black smudge against the dirty gleam of the tumbled river. It was moving very slowly for the wind was fighting for it with the stubborn tide. And in the boat she saw a standing figure, swaying as the boat rocked, leaning with one hand on some kind of staff, and waving the other with sweeping gestures in the air, as a man making a speech. As she looked a squall came over the water, a sudden gust of furious violence, as if the wind were seized with a passion of uncontrollable temper. The figure in the boat swayed backwards and recovered itself, and lurched forward and fell; it fell into the water with a great splash, which Margery saw, but never heard. Then she gave a wild, high cry. The wind caught it and flung it away, but many heard it. And none who heard it in all those houses will ever forget it. She ran crying up the garden, calling on the name of John Egerton. And John Egerton heard.

CHAPTER XVII

John Egerton came home very weary that evening; and all the way home things went wrong as they had gone wrong on a certain evening in June when he had come home tired to find the Byrnes' maid on the doorstep, and told the first lie about the sack. Tonight again the trains went wrong, and they were stuffy and packed, difficult to enter and difficult to leave and abominable to be in. It was one of the exceptional hateful journeys which men remember as they remember battles. It was of a piece with that night in June, and John thought of them together as he walked home, hot and jumpy with irritation. Nothing had gone right since that night – nothing. He had lost his love, and his good name, and his peace of mind – and his best friend. He had had faith in

Stephen then; he had admired and loved – had almost idolized him. Tonight he felt that he hated Stephen. Not a word from him – not one word of encouragement or gratitude in all this filthy business of the articles. Not that he wanted Stephen to *do* anything – oh no! He had made his vow and he would stick to it. But it did hurt that Stephen should take this sacrifice so much as a matter of course, should do nothing to help him in this new storm of suspicion. He had been a good friend once – a jolly, companionable friend, open-hearted and full of laughter – the best friend a lonely bachelor could have. Well, it was done with now. He had lost that he had lost everything else. And it had all begun with that lie. Perhaps it was a judgment. Perhaps there was never a virtuous lie.

He had bought at Charing Cross the October number of *The Argus*, because he had seen on the cover the name of Stephen Byrne, and he read everything that Stephen wrote. After dinner he sat down and read 'The Death in the Wood.' And at first he read, as Margery had read, only with admiration, thought it was now a jealous, almost reluctant admiration. He thought, 'How can a mean swine like Stephen create such glorious, high-minded stuff?' It was unnatural, wrong.

While he was reading the bell rang. Mrs

Bantam came in. 'It's them Gaunts,' she whispered. The Gaunt family had not been near him for months, and now they had come to pluck the certain fruit of the *I Say* articles. They stood in a defiant cluster in the tiny hall. John, for once, fortified and embittered by the exasperations of the Underground, allowed himself to be violently angry. He took a stick from the rack and shouted at them, 'Get out of my house – or I'll – I'll throw you out!' A little to his surprise they did go out, and he went back to 'The Death in the Wood,' pleasantly relieved by his self-assertion and anger.

He read on through the burial in the lake, and the finding of the maiden, and the battle at the lake where the faithful Tristram fought and was wounded. Then he came to the wooing in the castle, the false wooing by Gelert of Tristram's lady, the lovely Isobel. And here the soft heart of John melted within him; for the picture of Isobel which Stephen had drawn was so like the picture of Muriel that was ever in his own mind, a fair and gracious and relenting lady; and the hot words of Gelert were such words as he would have uttered and dreamed himself uttering, to Muriel Tarrant. But Muriel Tarrant had done with him, it seemed; she would hardly nod at him across the road; he had not spoken to her alone since that miserable dance. And this poetry of Stephen

Byrne's was the perfect expression of his faithful devotion, and made him almost weep with sentimental regret.

He read these passages several times. Then he went on to the poisoning by Gelert of Isobel's mind against her old lover, and his conquest of her, and his cruel desertion of her. And somewhere among those terrible lines the thought came to him as it had come to Margery, with a red-hot excruciating stab – that this story was a true story. And he looked back then, as Margery had looked, at the first pages of the poem and at the memory of those dreadful months in the new light of his suspicions. He remembered the dance, and Muriel's face at the dance; how kind at the beginning of it, how cold and cruel at the end – when she had danced many times with Stephen. He remembered how he had met her in September in the street; and how in her sidelong look there had been not only that coldness, but also a certain shame. Could it be...?

Once, he was sure, she had liked him a little – in the end he would have won her; she would have relieved him of this loneliness – this loneliness in an empty house with the hateful wind whining at the windows; but something devilish and unknown had got in the way... And if it was Stephen, and Stephen's lies... God! He would go to Muriel, he would go to Stephen; he would have it out of them, he would go now–

And as he paced up and down the room, working himself into a fever of rage, that terrible cry came out of the night, and he rushed out into the garden. Over the wall he scrambled to Margery, and heard her incoherent appeals; then on to Stephen's steps and down into Stephen's motor-boat. 'The oars,' he shouted – 'the oars!' and Margery pushed them, trembling, over the wall. He rowed out wildly towards the Island, missing the water and splashing emptily in his haste. He turned round, and there was nothing to be seen, no other boat, no bobbing head, – nothing, nothing but the gleam and shadow of the tumbled water. He rowed round laboriously in a wide circle for many minutes, peering, shouting, damp with spindrift and the sweat of rowing, though his hands were frozen and numb upon the oars. The boat was a hideous weight for rowing in the fierce wind, and when he could see nothing anywhere, he started the engine – with merciful ease – and steered up past the Island, since anything that was in the water must move up with the tide at last. The spray shot over the bows and blinded him. The boat steered drunkenly as he wiped his eyes and peered out at the water, and shouted weakly at the wind.

He came out past the Island into the open, and there he saw the dinghy, fifty yards ahead, a dark blot, dancing aimlessly sideways over the short waves. Anyhow, he would pick up the dinghy – it might be useful.

But when he came up with the dinghy he saw that there was something in it, something that was like the carved figures that may be seen brooding over tombs, with curved back and head drooping over clasped knees, a figure of utter dejection. But now and then it moved and paddled feebly in the water with one hand.

John called, with an incredulous question in his voice, 'Stephen? Stephen? Is that you?'

And it was Stephen, brooding bitterly over the shame of his last cowardice, and exhausted with the long struggle he had made for life. For the cold clutch of the water had woken up the love of life, and he had swum in a scrambling terror after the boat, and climbed with infinite difficulty back into the oarless boat. He was sodden and cold, and sick with humiliation. And John Egerton of all people must come and find him. So he turned his head and said with a great bitterness, 'O God! It's *you*, is it?'

When John saw that miserable figure, there began to take hold of him that old and fatal softness of heart; he felt very pitiful, and he said gently, 'Get in, Stephen.' And

Stephen crawled over into the other boat, the water streaming from him; and they sat together on the wide seat in front of the engine as they had sat so often before.

Then John said, 'What happened? We thought you–'

Stephen growled, 'So I did – but – but I funked it ... I was drunk.' Then he burst out, 'But, damn it, it's nothing to do with you... Turn her round – I'm soaked.'

And then, at the sullen bitterness of his voice and his words, John Egerton remembered his rage, he remembered the black grievance and suspicion he had against this man. And though the impulse to pity and forbearance struggled still within him, he fought it down. He would be firm for once. The boats swung sideways in the wind, and drifted, rolling, round the bend.

He put his hand behind him on the starting-handle of the engine, and he said:

'We're not going back yet, Stephen. I want to ask you something. What have you – what have you been – been doing to Muriel? What have you said to her – about me, and about–?'

'Oh, *hell*, John! I'm frozen, I can't sit jawing here. Start the boat and let me get home – or let *me*, damn you!' And he too seized the handle, gripping John's hand; and they sat there, crouching absurdly over the back of the seat, glowering at each other in the noisy wind.

And John nearly gave way; he felt that he was being unreasonable, perhaps foolish – this was no place for talk. But he was very angry and resentful again, and he had said he would be firm for once. And so do the tragedies of life have their birth.

He shouted, 'We're not going back till you've told me the truth – you've been telling lies to Muriel – you've made love to her. God knows what you've done – and you've got to tell me –*now!*'

'*Will* you let go of this handle, damn you? It's *my* boat!'

John held on. Then Stephen gave a great heave with his body, so that John nearly went overboard; but his grip held firm. So they fought with their bodies for a minute, heaving and panting and muttering low curses, and clutching still the disputed handle. The boat rocked dangerously, and the forgotten dinghy drifted away. They were beyond the houses now, and beyond the brewery, moving slowly past the flat and desolate meadows. There was no one to see them. But no one could have seen them. The rain was coming and it was really dark now; a huge black cloud had rolled up out of the west and blotted out the last stars. John looked once towards the meadows, but he could not see the bank – only a endless flickering blackness. They were alone out there in the howling dark, and they knew that they were alone. And at last, when nothing came of this insane struggle, Stephen suddenly took his hand from the handle and struck John a fierce blow on the side of the head; and John staggered, but gripped him immediately by the throat with his left hand, clinging still to the handle with his right. So they sat for a moment, Stephen clutching at the hand at his throat, and black hatred in the hearts of both of them, and their eyes fixed in a staring fury. Stephen was the stronger man, and with a supreme effort he tore away the hand from his throat. He dived forward over the thwart and seized one of the oars. Then he turned to attack, standing up in a crouching posture. But John Egerton had seen red at last, and he dimly knew that Stephen was yet more mad with fury than himself He had no weapon except the starting-handle in his hand, but as Stephen turned, he whipped this from its place and sprang forward; he struck out fiercely with the iron handle. Stephen lifted his oar to guard himself and the handle struck it with great force, with a heavy thud upon the wood. Stephen swayed a little, but he was unhurt, and the handle fell from John's hands into the boat. Then Stephen lifted his oar again and swung it in a wide circle, like a great sword, a vicious, terrible blow. But John

271

ducked, and it swept over his head. And while Stephen was yet recovering himself he sprang up, and he sprang at Stephen, and he lunged at him with his fist. John Egerton was no boxer, but fate was with him in that fight, and all the hoarded resentment of the summer was behind that blow. It caught Stephen on the point of the jaw as he raised his head. It caught him on the point of the jaw with the uncanny completeness of precision and force which no man can endure who is struck in that place. His head went up, and the oar dropped from his hands. For a moment he tottered, and then he fell, without a word, without a cry, forward and sideways, into the water. And John himself fell forward over the thwart, and lay panting in the rolling boat. When he looked out at last, he could see nothing, nothing but the empty water, and the empty meadows, and, far off, the lights of Barnes.

He searched the water for a long time, and after a little he found the oar, which Stephen had dropped; but he found nothing else. And at last he was sure that Stephen was dead. He went home slowly against the tide; and Margery was waiting in the garden, looking out into the wind. He told her simply that he could not find Stephen; and this time he lied easily.

That night she did not show him the paper

which she had found in the dining-room. But in the morning she gave it to him, and John tore it carefully into small pieces and threw them on the fire. And this he did without the sense or the circumstance of drama. For John Egerton was no artist. But he was a good man.

CHAPTER XVIII

So died Stephen Byrne. And the world talked for many days of the tragic accident of his drowning, of the tragic failure of his friend to find him, under the eyes of his wife, under the windows of his home. But the people of The Chase, at least, were not surprised; they had always said, they discovered, that he would overdo it at last ... pottering about on the river at all hours of night. They found the body, by a strange chance, among the thick weeds and rushes round the Island, about the place where Stephen had hunted for firewood on the last day. It had come down with the tide, and had been blown into the weeds, as the driftwood was blown. But the world did not know this, and they said it was the weeds which had pulled him down at last to his death.

Three weeks later the Stephen Byrne

Memorial Committee met for the first time. It was a truly representative body. Lord Milroy was, of course, in the chair, because he and Stephen were Old Boys of the same Foundation, and because he was always in the chair. John Egerton was a member because Margery insisted; and Dimple, Whittaker, and Stimpson represented The Chase with him. Indeed, the whole affair had its origin in The Chase. It was clear of course from the beginning that there would be a memorial somewhere, whether it was at Stephen's school or his birthplace; or it might even be a national memorial. But before anyone else had made a move the people of The Chase put their heads together and decided that it should be a Chase memorial, run by The Chase, and erected in or about The Chase. Further, in order to ensure that The Chase memorial should be *the* memorial, they astutely invited all possible competitive bodies to send representatives to sit on *The* Stephen Byrne Memorial Committee. All these bodies fell into the trap. The Old Savonians sent two representatives, and the village of Monckton Parva another; and a man came from the Home Office and another from the Authors' Society, and others from various literary bodies.

They met at the Whittakers', and Lord Milroy presided. Lord Milroy was one of those useful and assiduous noblemen who live in a constant state of being in the chair. One felt that at the Last Day he would probably be found in the chair, gravely deprecating the tone of the last speaker and taking it that the sense of the Committee was rather in favour of the course which commended itself to him. For although he was courteous and statesmanlike and suave, he was passionately attached to his own opinions, and generally saw to it that they prevailed.

On the matter of this memorial he speedily formed an opinion. There were many alternative proposals – some of them attractive, but expensive or impracticable, some of them merely fantastic. One man took the view that the work and character of Stephen Byrne would be most suitably commemorated by the endowment of a school of poetry in Northern Australia, where the arts were notoriously neglected. The school, of course, would bear the name of Stephen Byrne, and this would be a perpetual link between Australia and the mother country. The Old Savonians pointed out to the Committee that the gymnasium at Savonage, where Stephen Byrne had spent perhaps the happiest years of his life, must somehow be enlarged – if it was to keep pace with the expansion of the school. And the spirit of the founder's motto, 'Mens sana in corpore sano,' could hardly be so perfectly expressed as by the commemoration of a fine mind in the building up of fine bodies. Besides, there was no prospect otherwise of getting the gymnasium enlarged. The representatives of Monckton Parva were more ambitious. They said that the place where a man was born and the place where a man lived afterwards were the two great geographical monuments of his life. Since the Committee did not see their way to arrange for a memorial in each of these places, why not somehow unite them? The house where Stephen was born was now unhappily situated between a brewery and a tannery; and unless sufficient funds were subscribed to provide for the total destruction of the brewery and the tannery, the house as it stood could scarcely be regarded as a suitable nucleus for the memorial. They therefore suggested that the house should be demolished or rather disintegrated, brick by brick, and re-erected in a suitable site in Hammerton Chase as near as possible to Stephen's house. The house was small and comparatively mobile; indeed, there was a legend in the township that the house had been transplanted once, if not twice, already. Alternatively both the house at Monckton and the house at The Chase might be razed to the ground and re-erected as one building on a neutral site in Kensington, or perhaps Lincolnshire, a county which Stephen had mentioned very favourably in one of his poems.

Mr Dimple, who had been got at by the church, strongly advocated the claims of the Montobel Day Nursery; Stephen, he said, had had two children himself, and if he had been able to give an opinion, would almost certainly have elected to be commemorated by a gift to the little ones of the neighbourhood.

No one thought much of any of these suggestions; and after a great deal of bland and sugary argument the field of alternatives was thinned down for practical purposes to two – Mr Stimpson's plan and Mr Meredith's plan. Mr Meredith was the Home Office man. He had vacillated for a while between a Stephen Byrne monolith at Hammersmith Broadway and a Stephen Byrne Scholarship at London University, the balance of the fund to be devoted to the provision of a mural tablet in Hammerton church, setting out the principal works of Stephen Byrne, a kind of monumental bibliography. Finally, however, he decided in favour of the Hammersmith Broadway scheme. At that time there was much excitement in the Press over the conduct of foot passengers in the London streets, who were said to show an extraordinary carelessness of life in the face of the rapid increase of motor transport. For example, they took no notice of 'refuges';

they crossed the street at any old point. And Meredith's theory – which was also apparently the official theory of the Home Secretary, if not actually of the Home Secretary's private secretary – was that people neglected the refuges because they were such dull places. An unbeautiful lamp-post, he said, sprouting unnaturally from a small island of pavement, held out no inducement to pedestrians. It simply did not attract their attention, so they did not go there. Now, if they were made *attractive*, if every refuge at the principal crossings and danger-points were made into a thing of intrinsic beauty or interest, the people would crowd to them, to look at the statue, or read the inscription or drink at the fountain, or whatever it was. And he proposed that the first experiment should be made with a Stephen Byrne memorial at Hammersmith Broadway, which was very dangerous and had nothing striking in the centre of it. He said it was a curious thing that, if you counted the people who used the Piccadilly Circus refuge or the King Charles refuge in one day, you would find the number was 'out of all proportion' to the number of people who used an ordinary refuge where there was no fountain and no flower-girls and no statue of King Charles. Nobody could remember doing this, and very few of the Committee were prepared to take his word for it. In fact,

Stimpson said that what Meredith said was not borne out by his own experience (and this was as near as the Committee ever approached to open incredulity or contradiction); he also said that you do not *want* crowds gathering round refuges and gaping at pieces of sculpture; but then Stimpson was prejudiced, for Stimpson had his own plan.

And Lord Milroy came down heavily in favour of Stimpson's plan. He distrusted the Bureaucracy on principle and he disliked Meredith in particular. And he was not fond of John Egerton; John was another Civil Servant, and therefore a Bureaucrat, and John was the only member other than Meredith who was hotly opposed to Stimpson's plan. So that for a man less free from prejudice than the chairman there would have been a good deal of prejudice in favour of Stimpson's plan as against Meredith's plan.

And there was much to be said for Stimpson's plan. It had a certain imaginative boldness, and just that touch of sentiment which a memorial demands; and it was simple. He said that the great thing geographically in Stephen Byrne's life at Hammerton Chase was the river. He had loved the river; not Hammerton nor even The Chase, but the river. And any memorial that was made to him in Hammerton should be somehow

279

expressive of this. There was only one place where such a memorial could conveniently be made; and that place was the Island, the wild untenanted Island, the Island where he had died. At the eastern end of the Island, in sight of his own home, should his monument be put – a simple figure in some grey stone, sitting there in his favourite posture under the single willow-tree, with the knees drawn up and the head thrown back, and looking out with the poetic vision over that noble sweep of the wide river, at the gracious trees and delicate lights, and the huddled houses curving away... Stimpson was almost moving as he developed the idea, and most of the Committee were captivated at once. Lord Milroy said that he knew a sculptor who was the very man for such a task. He specialized in river-work; and Lord Milroy, when travelling in India, had been specially struck by a figure he had sc – by a figure looking over the Ganges, which was the work of this man. He also said that he was attracted by the breadth and freshness of the scheme; and this was true.

Only John Egerton hotly opposed it. The idea of a stone figure of Stephen Byrne, sitting for ever under the willow-tree in sight of his windows, and in sight of Margery's windows, revolted him. But he could think of no convincing objections. The Island was often submerged at high tide; the soil was sodden; the banks crumbled away. The land did not belong to Hammerton; nobody knew to whom it did belong, perhaps to the Port of London Authority, perhaps the Crown. Anyhow, it would take a long time to secure authority. And so on. His difficulties were easily dealt with; his timid suggestion that Margery might not like it was scornfully rejected: and after the chairman's summing-up, delivered in a very statesmanlike manner, the Committee by a large majority adopted the plan.

So, after many months, the statue was put up, and reverently unveiled. It was a noble piece of work. The figure was sitting in an easy posture on the thwart of a boat, and this rested on a low, broad pedestal that was just high enough to keep the figure out of the water at the highest tides, yet so low that you did not notice it. You looked over and saw simply the slight figure of a young man in grey, sitting near the water under a tree, his hands clasped about his knees, his feet crossed naturally, and his head thrown back a little, and his lips a little parted, as if he were asking some question of the things he saw. It was the exact posture of Stephen Byrne in that place, as many remembered it; and the tone and colour of the figure were so quiet and right that it was part of the scene, part of the river, and part of the

Island, as it was meant to be. And on the pedestal there was written, simply:

IN MEMORY
OF
STEPHEN BYRNE
A GREAT POET
HE LOVED THIS PLACE

The unveiling was a quaint, unusual ceremony. The time chosen was a little after high tide on a fortunate afternoon in early January, when the sun shone amazingly in a clear June sky, and the windless river wore its most delicate blue. There gathered round the draped figure at the end of the Island a splendid company of men and women. They came there necessarily in numbers of small boats, and the greater part of them remained all the time in these boats. They hung there in a dense crowd, clinging to ropes made fast to the Island. Only the Committee and the very great men stood on the Island by the tree. All those others, great and small, sat absolutely silent in their boats for many minutes; they had come long journeys, some of them, to see this thing, and some of them were only Saturday holiday-makers, brought there by curiosity as they rowed upstream; but they all sat silent. And as the hour for the unveiling came near, the tugs and the barges and the small boats

282

passing by stopped their engines or laid aside their sweeps or their oars, and stood still in reverence; and the river stood still, for it was slack water. All this quietness of respect was very moving; and the men and women rowed back afterwards in the warm sun, feeling that they had seen a fine thing.

It was marred only by one strange note. John Egerton and Margery did not go over for the unveiling; but they watched together from Margery's garden. And in the stillness there were many there who heard and remembered the high cackle of hysterical laughter which came over the water when the figure was revealed. It was a thin and horrible laughter that had no mirth in it, only a fierce and bitter derision. It went on for a full half-minute and faded away to a faint sound, as if the man laughing had gone suddenly into a house.

Muriel Tarrant heard it, for she was there with her mother, not in black, as were many of The Chase, but darkly dressed. When she heard that laughter she looked back quickly over her shoulder; and when she turned her head to the statue again, her face was very white.

Very soon the figure became a landmark to those who used the river. It became a mark among the watermen and bargees and the captains of tugs. And people made pilgrimages in small boats on the warm winter days to look at it and read the inscription.

Margery Byrne lived on in her house, and John Egerton lived on next to her in his. But why they stayed in that place it is hard to say. For you would think it was a cruel fate which set up at their own doors the graven image of their old idol; you would have said it was a hard thing to look out of the window at any hour of the day and see always some pilgrim at the shrine, doing his silent homage to the idol – gazing up from a boat or standing on the Island with his head bared – knowing nothing, suspecting nothing. And sometimes, indeed – they confessed to each other – they wanted to rush out to the river-side, and shout over the water at these worshippers the secret history of that splendid figure.

Yet it fascinated them. And it may be that, in spite of all, they were proud of it; they were proud in secret of the pilgrims and the homage and the Sunday crowds. It is certain at least that they never went to their beds – and this also they confessed to each other – they never went to their beds or threw up a window in the morning to bathe in the sun without turning their eyes up the river to the end of the Island, to the seated figure under the tree. On a dark night it was difficult to see, but on a moonlight night they could see it very clearly. And they looked at it always. The idol had something still of the old magic, though they knew that the feet of it were clay. But on the wild sou'wester nights they looked out very quickly and drew close the blinds. And on those nights they were always sad.

But the statue stood there for three months only. In April there was a great storm and a great tide. The wind and the rain came violently out of the south-west and beat upon the statue; and the swollen tide rushed up over the Island, and over the road, and over the little gardens of The Chase; it surged up about the knees of the statue, and tugged and fretted at the crumbling banks. At dusk the tide was not full, but already the short waves were slapping the face of the statue, and there was nothing to be seen under the willow-tree but the head and shoulders of a man struggling in the furious race of the flood. In the morning it was seen that the bank and the new stone facing of the bank had collapsed; and at low tide the statue was found grovelling in the mud, with its nose shattered. The willow is very near to the edge of the Island now, and it is strange that it survived that tide. There is nothing under it now but a small patch of rich green grass, very noticeable from the windows of the Terrace. This grass is a favourite haunt of the Island swans; and they stand there for hours, cleaning themselves.

So for the first time the true story of

Stephen Byrne is told; and those at least who live in The Chase will know the real name of Stephen Byrne and the real name of Hammerton Chase. It is to be hoped that they will be kinder now to John Egerton, and as kind as they can be to the memory of Stephen Byrne. For there is something to be said for every man; and Stephen Byrne was a strange mixture.

As for the rest, the pilgrims and the far worshippers they may understand the story or they may not; and it can be no great matter to them. For they never knew Stephen Byrne in the flesh; and they have his poetry as they had it before. And when the statue is put back securely in its place, no doubt they will come to see it again. For, after all, the inscription said that he was a great poet; it did not say that he was a good man.

The publishers hope that this book has given you enjoyable reading. Large Print Books are especially designed to be as easy to see and hold as possible. If you wish a complete list of our books please ask at your local library or write directly to:

Dales Large Print Books
Magna House, Long Preston,
Skipton, North Yorkshire.
BD23 4ND

This Large Print Book, for people
who cannot read normal print,
is published under the auspices of

THE ULVERSCROFT FOUNDATION